MY DARK

Frank Delaney was born in Tipperary, Ireland in 1942. After an early career in banking, much of it spent in Dublin, he became a broadcaster with RTE, the Irish national radio and television network. In 1975 he began work as a freelance contributor and documentary programme maker for the BBC in Northern Ireland. He has lived in London since 1978, originated the Radio 4 programme *Bookshelf*, wrote and presented features, talks and documentaries – both for radio and television – and the *Frank Delaney* series on BBC2. He is married to the designer Susan Collier.

ARENA
NOVELLA

MY DARK ROSALEEN

Frank Delaney

ARENA
NOVELLA

An Arena Book
Published by Arrow Books Limited
20 Vauxhall Bridge Road, London SW1V 2SA

An imprint of Random Century Group

London Melbourne Sydney Auckland
Johannesburg and agencies thoughout the world

Originally published in the Hutchinson Novella series
General Editor: Frank Delaney
First published by Hutchinson 1989

Arena edition 1990

Typeset in Lasercomp Photina by
Vision Typesetting, Manchester

Printed and bound in Great Britain by
The Guernsey Press Co. Ltd, Guernsey, Channel Islands

ISBN 0 09 9 70670 9

In memory of A.L. – and for M.J.

Prologue

I am beached. Stranded between the high ground of what I think is right and what others would determine for me – a common complaint, and rampant on this island. I sit in my car beside this undistinguished shore, with white shale sloping up towards the dunes, scrabgrass in spikes. You can see this peninsula on the map, a long, narrow point in the south-east. The ocean lies due south, and west; to the east a lesser sea, behind me the land. The lighthouse men have a saying, 'The land is the danger.' How right they are.

In a few hours I have to meet some men here, and I am shaking.

Several weeks ago I became involved in a local incident which grew into a national scandal, a front-page story, an outcry; now it threatens me vitally, though none of it was of my doing, not any of it. But I made an error of faith – my usual one: I confused idealism with how things really are. Not my fault, I claim. Blame my heritage. Blame the politics, the political atmosphere into which I was bred.

You see, the new State was less than ten years old when I was born, and patriotism still flourished. Mournful old tales, sad or rebellious ballads, local heroes, hedgerow warriors – the place echoed with the dying gunshots of revolution. At last we ruled our own destiny. Thus we had the glorious struggle to remember and the political freedom to enjoy it. And we listened to speeches and sermons telling us that we were new, the Risen People. We had come from a long and wonderful ancestry, rich and ancient; and now, in charge of ourselves, we would be upright. Moral. Pure. And strong.

I believed it, too. I learned the words by heart, chanting them along with the others, those words of our Leader – 'The Chief', they called him – who had looked into his heart and found the vision he was creating for us. We wrote out his sentences as headlines in our school copybooks, as exercises:

> 'The home of a people who valued material wealth only as the basis of right living, of a people who were satisfied with frugal comfort and devoted their leisure to the things of the spirit – a land whose countryside would be bright with cosy homesteads, whose fields and villages would be joyous with the sounds of industry, with the romping of sturdy children, the contest of athletic youths and the laughter of comely maidens, whose firesides would be the forums for the wisdom of serene old age. It would, in a word, be the home of a people living the life that God desires man should live.'

We listened. And we learned – the old native language, and the legends of the warriors, the giants striding the hillsides, and the songs from the days when our forefathers were not allowed to mention the country by name, so gave her the name of a loved woman. We were taught *Oh My Dark Rosaleen, do not sigh do not weep. The priests are on the ocean green. They march along the deep.*

It was a love-song – the love of our country, for which brave men fought and died. I learned every verse of that and I sang its melancholy air at parties – with a little introduction, perfectly rehearsed.

Where I really went wrong, though, was in my belief that the goodness, the probity hurled daily from platform and pulpit really existed. That nationally we had come within an ace of that brilliant stainlessness, that this was part and parcel of the same revolutionary ideal, moral as well as political freedom. All right, I was naive, I lived in fantasy; but I was not alone. I was encouraged – by my teachers, by my parents, by my society – and so was all my generation. Perhaps I was one of those many who never grew up. 'A prig' – that is what Hennessy, the lawyer they gave me, said. 'Do you know what a prig is, Mr Newman? It is a pain in the arse, that is what a prig is.' Well, he is entitled to his opinion.

The beach is empty, the tide coming in. Next month it fills to the highest of the year, a spring-tide. Local people, getting it wrong, call it 'the neap': trust them to call the highest the lowest.

What time is it? Five o'clock. I have a few more hours before they arrive. 'So that you can make the right decision,' they said. 'For your own good.'

In the quiet, here, I can sit and think. My head, on one side, still hurts occasionally, especially when I am tired: heavy blows, stone-hard fists. I have used the time well, though; I wrote it all down, the whole fearful story, and how it happened. Hennessy has a copy – his idea. 'Just in case,' he said. 'Just in case . . .'

1

Saturday 13 June, 1959, a rainy day. I left the town in the early afternoon. The bank closed at half-past eleven and I balanced my cash – we never had more than a few customers on a Saturday. Everybody knows everybody else in this town, a square of old shops and tall houses, and a clock on the wall of the post office, and wharves, some redundant bulwarks, by the Causeway leading to the Atlantic. Married cousins and private maiden ladies and misfits live here, and returned emigrants and cripples, and smart talkers and cool guessers, and crooks and crocks and hypocrites, and gents and spinsters and fools, and hopers and no-hopers, and givers and takers and movers and shakers, and milkers and gleaners and lifters and leaners and grafters and shafters. In other words, an average populace. They walk through the door with their money in American cheques, or biscuit tins, or cash from cattle marts or the creamery cheques – what we call 'the farmer's salary'.

I am the cashier, 'a profession for gentlemen', I was informed when I joined, and my colleagues will all tell you, a little pompously, that we are Bank Officials, not bank clerks, and that we don't have managers and assistant managers, we have Agents and Sub-Agents, since the days when some local big-wig was invited to be 'the Agent for the Bank'. I am a stranger here, from a hundred and fifty miles away in the West: bank policy, so that local secrets are not known to local people. I took an oath of secrecy when I joined, the Bible in my hand as I stood in front of the Chief of Establishments at Head Office. Today I am wearing a sports jacket and grey trousers, on weekdays we wear suits, and only on Saturdays are we allowed to wear collar-attached shirts. The Agent owns a yellow knitted waistcoat he wears on Saturdays beneath his sports jacket, and a tweed tie.

I locked the bank door behind me and said hello-goodbye to the chemist standing at her door next door. The way out of the town wound up a steep hill past the cemetery, the site of an ancient battle, the spires of the town in the distance behind. The car, bought out of my Relief Staff expenses, could hardly make it. Thorn branches and rain swatted the windscreen; the trees facing in from the sea hunched away from the winds. Last night was tough: hard going – the drinking went on till all hours. My face hurts, I feel white aureoles around my eyes and eyebrows. Last night Affectionate Pat, polishing the counter, said death was in the air. I drank too much. I have no money left and I will have to pay him the week after next when the salary cheque comes in from Head Office. Affectionate Pat won't mind: he loves the power.

He leaned over to me and said, 'There'll be no singing tonight, laddo.'

'Why, Pat? What's the score?'

'Morose, that's why. Everyone's in real bad form.'

'Ah, go on. Is that the way it is with you, Pat?'

'Not with me. With the air.' He waved upwards. 'I can always tell when something bad is going to happen.'

He patted my arm affectionately. That is why he was

called Affectionate Pat.

'Ah, go on, Pat.'

'No. God's honest truth. Always tell.'

He leaned across the mahogany and looked right and left as if a vehicle might be coming down the counter. But it was just one of Pat's little anecdotes, heading our way.

'When I was in *there* . . .' This is the wink, the intimacy, this is how he makes people pay for their free drinks. Affectionate Pat did time in a seminary trying to be a priest. Great wonders and unspeakable failures took place in *there*. Quiet, useless prostrations occurred in candlelight. All to no avail; Affectionate Pat came out as unordained as he went in. 'Spoiled' is the word they use, 'a spoiled priest'. His lips are always wet.

'When I was in *there*' means the seminary; sometimes he calls it 'the quare place' or 'the hostelry' or, in one odd fit, 'the sanctity bin', letting slip for an instant his demeanour which he had brought to the same polish as his bald and shiny head.

'When I was in there a fellow cut his throat. He had this habit. Every night he'd strop his razor. Last thing at night. *Tchev-Tchev. Tchev-Tchev*. Now this one week I smelt death in the air. Don't you know? Mind you, I'd been keeping an eye on this laddo. Anyway, this night, this one night he did it. He stropped the razor, an old cut-throat, as per usual. *Tchev-Tchev. Tchev-Tchev*. Well, whatever look I gave, the lights were still on, the man next to him gets up and switches off the lights. So I gave another look, I thought something funny, and so did the man alongside him and after about five minutes up I gets, and over to the lights and switches them on and out jumps the man longside our friend and sees him hunched

13

up in the bed and goes over and puts his fingers into the huge gash our friend has made in his own throat. *Tchev-Tchev*. Right. Coming. How are you, Jer? A small one, how's the boys?'

Affectionate Pat went away in pursuit of his new customer, and, as ever, gave his *denouement* time to enjoy itself. He came back and said, 'Well, anyway can't you imagine? Pandemonium. Ree Raw and rooilleh-booilleh. And grief. The gods insulting with superior strength. Fell heavy on him. Palinurus, don't you know?'

Another thing about Affectionate Pat, he always gives his sources. Saves you looking them up, and never permits you to forget he had a seminary education.

'Not far from here, either. Big funeral, we all went, huge funeral. Sang the *Dies Irae*. The whole shooting gallery. Sung Office and Requiem Mass. The mother apparently was the problem, a bit sanctimonious, don't you know the way they are, always praying and a tongue on her at the same time that would lift the tar off the roads. Always sighing and wondering would he have the guts to stay and be ordained. Only your man couldn't take it. Near Easter, this was, so we all broke up, extra two or three weeks. Anyway we came back and can't you imagine what it was like in that dormitory? Huh, ho, nervous, boy, out-and-out nervous.' With sweeping hands he polished the counter.

'Everyone undresses. Silently enough. Odd nervous joke here and there, don't you know, lights out, switched them off myself. Well, I own to God, no sooner were we in the beds and all lying still, than some genius quietly begins to strop his razor in the dark, *Tchev-Tchev, Tchev-Tchev*. There you are now. Hee-hee. Hello Rose, and fresh and well you're looking the night.'

The rain stopped, the windscreen cleared. A woman on a bicycle, head down against the wind, going opposite, into town, saluted. Past a large stud farm, white railings and a winding drive, a big-windowed house. I did not go to bed until four, oh, Jesus my head and eyes, and how I drove the car back to the lodgings I will never know. The lights were out even on the Causeway. In the window of the paper shop Eisenhower's photograph reminded me and I have to thank Affectionate Pat for the idea. In the village of Bane lives a man who has come back from America with a pile, 'a huge pile', says Pat, the authority on such matters, of jazz records. Jazz and traditional music, not much to separate them, all up to the individual. On the road a woman put up her hand for a lift; the same woman, Rose O'Mara, who had come in last night, except that she left a long time before me, and with somebody, because I had eyed her. I stopped just beyond her and she caught up.

'Oh, hello. Any chance of a lift?'

'Hop in. Where are you going?'

'Over to the teacher's in Bane. He has to sign a form for me.' I said that was where I was going too, not to the teacher's but to Bane.

I saw her last night all right, and I connected. And also connected now; I had 'Thoughts', a priest at school called them. 'Beware, dear boys, of impure thoughts and occasions of sin.'

Preened and groomed she was. Got ready in the late morning.

In her slip and lipstick bedroom. A good wash, first, a good

15

wash, you know, empty the basin in the yard afterwards. Soft light of June in the room, slim sunbeams, dusty light. Rising off one heel, lift off one buttock, then turn, and the other, quick and gentle inspection, with pursed lips, and hair falling sheeny to neck. The soft domes and cones, the sweet fat peaks and shadows. I could see her. Thoughts.

Smelling of such things, she settled large in the little leather seat beside me.

'You're lucky to have a car.'

'Oh, yes?'

'I'd love to have one. You know. For going out an evening.'

The image bends and swims. Bulkily downward she reaches, to fetch cotton and satin, white and flesh-coloured, from the drawer beneath the mirror. In the bedroom now the honey light has shafted slowly around, the haunches creased by drawing on stockings. She sits on a cheap pink quilt, legs raised a little, plump there and amiably apart.

And now I have to clear my throat, is this an occasion of sin? Thoughts . . .

She said, 'I saw you in The Enterprise last night.'

'Yes.'

'He's a talker, isn't he?'

'Who?'

'Who else? Affectionate Pat.'

'Ah, yes, he's a talker all right.'

'Were you late?'

'A cop wouldn't ask that question.'

'Ah, no. I didn't mean –'

'Only joking. I was very late. Half-three. Four.'

'Jesus. That's what you'd call late. I'd be killed if I came in that late. Jimmy'd have a fit. Waking the house.'

16

'Who's Jimmy?'

'The husband.'

'You must be frightened of him?'

'No, I am not,' she said. 'He's a quiet enough fella. 'Tis just that I like to keep him that way. The quiet life, you know.'

'Are you often out late?'

She looked over slyly. 'Go on now. Why were you so late, anyway?'

'Ah, Pat was gloomy.'

'Not like him. He's usually too cheerful, if anything.'

'Ah, he was going on.'

'About what?'

'About death. Superstitious. You know.'

'Funny, he was on about that to someone else. Not last night – the night before. What did he mean by it at all?'

'Well, he said it was somebody going to get killed.'

'Jesus, I hope 'tisn't me. Are you a good driver?'

'Don't worry. This thing couldn't go that fast.'

' 'Tis a car, though.'

'On – its – last – legs' – said in clunking time with a gear change down this steep hill.

'D'you want a cigarette?' she asked.

'No, thanks. I'm burnt out. Too many last night.'

'You're in the bank, aren't you?'

'How d'you know that?'

'I saw you at the Hunt Dance. You were pointed out to me.'

'And your name –?'

'Mrs O'Mara. When things are formal I'm Rosaleen. And the rest of the time they call me Rose.'

17

A blouse, then a skirt, and Rose stands up to zip. Hand flashes in to settle strap, and in profile the domes are hefted, both hands, more in assurance than necessity. Dimmer in the room now, as Rosaleen leaves, collecting her handbag from the bed and closing the door tidily behind her.

I turned my mind back to the road.

She asked, 'I suppose you have a wife?'

'No.'

'Why so?'

'On the road too much, always transferred. Relief staff.'

'No girl anywhere?'

'A few.'

'One in every port?'

'That's the way.'

'But you're permanent here.'

'Sort of. For the last year and a half.' Could I drive with these 'thoughts'? How often, my son, do you have impure thoughts? Sometimes, Father. And everywhere I look the thoughts follow me – even down to her red shoes, thin leather strap high around her ankle. I read in a magazine somewhere, at the barber's, I think, that 'sling-back heels have become the natural successors to the ankle bracelet of the harlot'.

'What forms are you getting signed?'

'A grant. For an extension.'

'Big house?'

'No. There's only the two of us.'

'No children?'

'Not a one. Just myself and Jimmy.'

'How long are you married?'

'Twelve years. I'm working.'

'What has that to do with children?'

'You're very forward.' Looking straight ahead. A drag on the cigarette, a breath of smoke. The smoke and the perfume – or is it hair lacquer, or is it talcum powder? Woolworths.

'I can't have children. If you want to know.'

'That. Ah. Must.'

'Must what?'

'Nothing.' I stopped speaking and she looked ahead. She sat back. She opened the tie belt of the white coat, drew on the cigarette and asked, 'Aren't you a bit forward altogether?'

Yes, all right, a bit forward: my 'thoughts' had eased up a little, though the ache of them still sat around.

'What do you do?'

'How d'you mean?'

'What are you working at?'

'Hairdressing. Hair by Liam on Cliff Street.'

'I must go in for a perm,' I said.

'Far from perms you were reared.'

She dragged on the cigarette.

I said, 'Did you hear the news on the wireless last night?'

'No, but everybody's talking about it. About Eisenhower, d'you mean?'

So I told her. The announcer said, 'Hundreds of thousands of West Berliners lined the streets of their native city today as President Eisenhower arrived. They greeted him with American flags and flowers and shited "Ouk! Ouk!" I beg your pardon, that should be "and shited Ouk! Ouk!"

19

'Once more he said it, "And shited Ouk! Ouk!" What he meant was "and shouted Ike! Ike!"'

She laughed and coughed with the laughing, and I laughed too.

Out to our left the headland rose away in meadows from the sea, and the sun grew stronger. The car warmed, the leather seats shone in the sunlight. She said, 'I think I'll take off my coat.' Thrusting herself forward in the seat, she eased the coat off her shoulders. She wore a red jumper tight enough across her prow and then she lurched off one hip, then the other, to get the coat out from under her. The skirt creased into the vale of her lap.

The landscape in which I grew up, and in which I roamed and dreamed, had lakes and wet marshlands and still a few wild ponies and many, many rocks. I wondered what creatures – dragons, gorgons – dwelt inside, in the hearts of the rocks. The pools grew heathers and wavy weeds; a few trees hung by our house, giving it a little shelter. The nearest neighbours – farmers – lived half a mile away, elderly, a brother and sister. I took some parenting from them: he, gross and half-blind, invited me on expeditions to buy cattle, or parts of tractors, or the long, toothy blades for mowing machines; she, sweet-faced and generous, gave me biscuits and lemonade.

I grew up alone, more or less, used the footwork of domestic unobtrusiveness and diligent homework to avoid my parents' tense and sullen attentions, read every book I could find, lived in my dreams, paid for my schooling with scholarships and rejected a university place in order to get away from home. I think about that sometimes. I could have had a music scholarship, they said at school. 'Perfect pitch,' they said and a natural affinity with harmony; not a composer but perhaps an exciting and individual interpreter. They tried to ease me away from traditional music, Bach, they said, he was the man. However, up the road, in the churchyard, lay Carolan's grave, this blind harper who went across the rainy countryside on a white horse, led by a servant, welcomed at great houses, given damp beds in draughty rooms.

I suppose, not to be too grand about it, I am a bit of a journeyman too. I will go back on the Relief Staff soon, and I will go on travelling from town to town counting the people's money and singing at their parties. They say to me, 'You have a lovely voice. Lovely and true.' At which I smile, because I know this, and I also know that I do not fit in with them. Not their fault: I have no training, given the household I came from, for fitting in with people, my exterior is acquired and I have enough of it to let me count their cash and address them in lonely old songs.

Beside me she coughs, lifts an arm to smooth back her hair and her smell expands in the heat of the sun in the car.

'Heavy smoker?'

'How do you know? The cough?'

'Yeah. Real graveyard job.'

'Only on wet mornings.'

'What does your husband do?'

'He works at the creamery. A separator.'

'He lets you out a lot?'

'I go out a lot.'

21

'Doesn't he go with you?'

'Sometimes.'

'So you're a free agent?'

'I'm always a free agent.' She sat up forward suddenly. 'Oh, look, there's Henry Mac. Can you give him a lift? Have you room?'

'Plenty of room for decent people.' I pulled up. We were trained by the bank in what they called 'character assessment', whether people were trustworthy. 'Face value may be full value,' the instructor warned. 'Integrity is the best collateral.' Would I lend to this man, Henry Mac? On face value? Yes and no. He looked like a cat kept at court, sleek and elderly and feigning.

'Hallo, Henry. How's the form? Are you going somewhere, d'you want a lift?'

'How are you, Rose? You're looking good. And who is the gentleman? You had a different boy with you the last time.'

'Ah, would you stoppit, Henry? This man is giving me a lift over to Bane. You know him, don't you? You surely know his face – out of the bank, you know.'

'A man with money. A Midas touch. How are you?' He shook hands with me. 'What's your name?' I had to turn fully around, right hand over left shoulder, to shake his hand. He sat forward, leaning on the seats, his head occupying the area between Rose and me.

'Newman.' I took back my hand: seventy if he was a day.

'Mr Newman. You're a gentleman and a scholar.'

'And a judge of good whiskey,' she said. 'You're always saying that, Henry. Where are you going?'

'Well now, I don't want to be in the way,' he said, 'of

you young people.'

'Ah, would you stoppit, Henry? Mr Newman and I are only met this minute. He gave me a lift on the road.'

'Then Mr Newman is a decent man for giving people lifts.' He sat back in the rear seat. 'The truth of the matter, Rose, is that I don't know where I'm going, and that, Mr Newman, has been my guiding sentiment throughout this weary life.'

'Will you listen to him?' She turned to face him, thereby moving her body three-quarter ways towards me. Did you commit any impure actions, my child? Sometimes, Father.

'You don't have to worry, Henry, with all your money. He has pucks of it' – this last remark towards me.

'I'm trying to place your accent,' I said to him, 'Mr Mac . . .'

'The name I most appreciate is Henry Mac, full Henry Mac. My intimates, like Rose here – isn't that right, Rose, to call you an intimate? – call me Henry. I like Henry Mac myself, the full whack, Henry Mac and no "Mr" to a decent man like yourself, Mr Newman, and now you'll have a job to trace my accent, I have been all around the world and back and my accent, rather military I suppose you think, is decorated with curlicues and frizzles from everywhere, Bali to Belmullet, Rhodesia to Rathfarnham.'

'A man of the world, is that what you are?'

'Takes one to know one, Mr Newman.'

'Henry, you didn't tell me.'

'Tell you what, Rose? That you are as beautiful and as fresh as the day itself?'

'No. Where you're going.'

'I'm easy. I'm a little breathless after a long appointment early this morning. With my solicitor.'

'Did you get good news itself?'

'No, Rose, my dear girl. Solicitors only give you bad news, you make good news for them. Rose, have you by any chance a cigarette?' He leaned forward with a cigarette holder which he had taken from his top pocket and had fitted together as thoughtfully as an assassin might assemble a gun.

'Henry, you're a scream. All that money and you're walking the roads and borrowing cigarettes.'

'In answer to your question I am as you will guess bound homewards, and you two people and you indeed Mr Newman must come, have a drink or a late lunch with me.'

'He has a lovely house,' Rose added.

'Have you the time for a civilised drink, Mr Newman?'

'I drank a lot last night.'

'Then you will need a cure.'

'What about you?' I said sideways to her. 'Haven't you an appointment?'

'No. He said any time today would do. I rang him from the Post Office.'

'I'm in the same boat,' I admitted. 'No fixed time. And 'tis Saturday.'

'The day of the gods,' said Henry.

'Right, Henry. You're on,' said Rose.

'Oh good. Thank you both. You will help to allay my feelings of impending doom.'

Him too. The car fell silent. He had thrown the remark away but it had fallen in my direction. Apprehension. My old friend. The acid in my mother's voice or my father's

24

surly truculence. Apprehension for my sister, returning from college, to face scathing comment upon her clothes, on her lipstick, on her friends. No wonder she stopped going home. Apprehension for my poor uncle, who had a most beautiful, bass voice, the musical gene, but who had to live in fantasy to escape the sarcasm of his family, and who spun stories for us, of his days as a merchant seaman fighting the Lascars on the quays at Marseilles – he who had never been to sea – of racing the storms to haven in Port of Spain. Among these tales he lived, coming out only to sing solo in church at Christmas or for the Archbishop, or a few times with visiting orchestras in the city. My mother's embarrassed abuse of him reached a high pitch – 'that fool', she would say in his hearing, or to his wife, or to his daughters, 'that imbecile', or 'that clown with that ridiculous voice of his.' He eventually took a most logical course: he went deaf and for the rest of his life went around in a happy, half-smiling silence, hearing no more abuse, singing in his head no doubt notes as profound as the ocean, full fathom five his troubles lay buried, never to rise again, silence his weapon against being shamed.

'Turn to your left soon, Mr Newman, next left for my humble abode.' Henry Mac spoke his clichés as if they were verses.

Rose and Henry Mac had been engaged in earnest conversation about discretion. He had been saying, 'it's a small town, Rose, and people talk,' and she had been saying, 'they don't talk as much as you think; too many of them can't afford to talk,' and he had been saying, 'the women talk, Rose,' and she with her coughing laugh had been saying, 'Henry, it's not the women I worry about,' and he had been saying, 'Oh Rose, you are a character,' and she said, 'they can't say much here, Henry; sure they're all related to each other,' at which point he told me to turn left.

A small bridge on the long drive jolted the car and the trees dripped; large drops and small leaves. Under the ivy the seat curved in front of the bow window. The gravel ran into the grass of large lawns and the air had the sweetness of nearby gardens: I neither locked the car nor took the key from the ignition; nobody who lived here had any need to steal a car. Exactly two, chimed a clock somewhere, permitting Henry to say, 'The sun's well over the yardarm. No excuse.' He waved us towards the front door with its bootscrapers, and on the way he turned to me and added, 'Mr Newman, I do not wish to presume further upon your decency, but perhaps you might sing for me, for us, later?'

I stepped back a little, and began to say, 'Ah, well . . . the thing, you see . . .' then as it struck me I said, 'How do you know I sing?' He simply replied with authority, 'It would be a great favour,' and in the hallway opened a door to a room which contained a baby grand piano, a harp and several other musical evidences.

I said, 'Of course I will. Yes.'

Rose, her coat splayed on an ottoman, stood in the hallway. 'Look at this.' She pointed to a large waving-hands statue, a predictable goddess, though of jade. 'Worth a fortune, Henry says. We're to go in here.' I have been in quite a few houses like Henry Mac's: the lesser ones have faded, their owners unable to continue with high levels of maintenance, or uninterested in keeping the house's traditions alive. Those which have been well-

26

loved, like this one, still have all their gracious features. Why, then, was I uneasy? While he had been in my car I was the host, he was in my control. No longer.

In a small panelled room with many books stood Henry, beside the window overlooking a long terraced garden. 'Madge will be here, I've rung the bell, you will have lunch. Champagne or spirits, Mr Newman? You need a cure? Champagne? Good, good, and Rose, my dear, a lady must never refuse champagne.'

He poured nothing for himself. 'I look on in silent pleasure while people drink.'

She, who had taken a gulp, said, 'Henry killed somebody once, didn't you, Henry? Common knowledge. Come on, Henry. You told me it was the reason you didn't drink.'

'Yes, it is true, Rosaleen, but I do not see why Mr Newman should be burdened with it. Madge' – he spoke to the housekeeper, then turned to me – 'We have half an hour to lunch; would you like to see the house? I have a rather nice gallery, Victorian accretion.'

'And not chick nor child to leave it to,' said Rose. 'Have you made the will yet, Henry?' He leaned across to her and kissed her on the cheek, allowing his hand to touch a breast. 'Dear Rose. We must talk.'

As we passed through the hall, and again into the music room, I felt something with which I am familiar and which I fear. I am prone to a kind of wildness; feelings overcome me and I grow reckless, make utterly indiscreet remarks. I think it's usually caused by extreme anxiety. When it hits me, I do dangerous things. In particular, I invent totally untrue stories about people, stories which are not only totally untrue, but which can easily be checked and easily proven, without any doubt, to be untrue. On such occasions I get into trouble – with the wives of other men, with bank colleagues, with chance acquaintances in bars. Now I felt it come over me again, and for once I had sufficient composure to acknowledge it and find a way to check it. The way to deal with it is to become extra-polite and to get away for a moment or two. Besides, Rose had her arm around Henry's waist.

I said, 'May I go back into the music room for a moment?'

Henry Mac, behind me now, said, 'Yes, I have neglected Rose a little. And why don't you warm up, they tell me you have a lovely voice.'

The song came up in my head. *Oh my Dark Rosaleen, do not sigh do not weep. The priests are on the ocean green. They march along the deep.* I sat at the piano. Some scales. Doh, Ray, Me, Fah, Soh, Lah, Tee, Doh. Tonic Sol-fa. Silence, suddenly in the house, a huge house, a huge silence. Keep the wildness at bay. Whatever you say say nothing. Through the long window I saw a horse grazing. The hard rain had ended, the summer had returned, the afternoon would grow hot. Large elms marched down the fields: was this one of those houses that celebrated Wellington's victory at Waterloo by planting regiments of trees? So Henry killed somebody, did he? And why the car in the garage if he walks the roads? I saw it, to one side, as we drove in. And how did he know that I sang? I heard a little moan above my head. I knew the reason for my wildness; apprehension, as well as anxiety. I am being manipulated. Made a witness. To his powers. But he must be seventy, at least. On the piano a photograph sat in a leather frame: 'Henry and Robert at Trinity 1900, the Century Ball'. God – eighty. Say he was twenty then, born 1880 – well, seventy-nine at least. Jesus. The old ram. The gong rang. Peevish, I waited for him to fetch me, I did not, after all, know where to go. The housekeeper, Madge, did, 'In here, sir.' Amazingly, they sat there already. He dapperly rose and expanded to welcome and seat me, holding the napkin in front of his tweed crotch, but that is where I annoy myself, looking for clues where people are not trying to hide something. And in any case she, Rose, had unprecedented – as far as my brief knowledge of her was concerned – unprecedented colour in her cheeks, and when he had engaged with the food she winked at me, and with her plump slash of a mouth puffed me a small kiss. My wildness flared again. There's wine from the Royal Pope. Upon the ocean green. And Spanish ale shall give you hope. My Dark Rosaleen.

After the food I sang for them, in the music room. The same song. I prefaced it, as I usually do, with my famous well-rehearsed remarks: 'In the Penal Days, when our Earls had fled to France, and our forefathers were not allowed to love their country, they referred to the country as a woman. They gave her various names, pet names, "Kathleen the daughter of Houlihan", or "The Old Woman of Beare" or "The Little Black Rose". The Poet, James Clarence Mangan, translated the old song, "Little Black Rose", and it was called "My Dark Rosaleen", and was set to a traditional air.' And I sang it. 'Oh my dark Rosaleen, do not sigh do not weep. The priests are on the ocean green. They march along the deep.' I gave them four verses, ending with, 'Would give me life and soul anew, A second life, a soul anew, My Dark Rosaleen!'

'Bravo! Bravo!' Full of feeling, Henry said to me, 'Mr Newman, you are very good. You are very good indeed. You are superb. Oh, it's right what they say, you have a true voice.'

I blushed, I think.

He asked, 'Any training?'

'No.'

'Shame that, though it might spoil the natural, the – how shall I put it? – the *naïf* quality. No offence, of course, the contrary, the contrary. I could pay for your training.'

'No. No. Not at all. Thanks. No.'

'Yes, a man has his pride. Well, well. The singing bank clerk. My word.'

He shook his head. 'What do you say to that, Rosaleen? Have you ever heard a song sung so beautifully?'

Rose, uninterested and yawning, said, 'My father used to sing that. D'you know any Country and Western?'

'Now,' Henry said, 'I will play for you', and in my egotism and wildness I had thought of the music room as only something he had inherited and had kept up for the sake of decoration. 'Schubert,' he said, 'an impromptu, what else?' And he played excellently. When he had ended, as I seemed about to applaud, he placed a finger to his lips, sat in the silence he had created for several seconds, then stood up very quietly. Controlling. He came across to the chair on which I sat, bent down beside me and whispered, 'I am going for a *siesta*, never lost the habit. Call me in an hour and do not go without me.' No question that I might argue with him. Then he left the room. I sat looking out through the long window at the horses in the field.

Rosaleen started awake, looked at me and said, 'Where's the oul' fella gone?'

'Upstairs. For a rest. An hour. He wants us to wait – not to go without him.'

'All right.'

'I'm anxious to go.'

'No, hold on. He's a useful man. He'll pay for everything.'

'He's a dangerous man.'

'Dangerous? Henry, is it? How can you say that? Henry isn't dangerous. Henry's all right. Wait till you get to know him.'

She rose from the couch, stood in front of the window and said, 'C'mon. Up this way.'

'Where are you going?'

'Up. Come on.'

At the top of the stairs, facing the staircase, the wide bathroom door stood open. Inside, on the far wall, hung a painting of two musicians, a lutanist and a girl playing a reed pipe: Dutch. The room, wide and bright, overlooked the drive. The bath stood in the middle of the floor, large and, surprisingly, steaming, full of recently-run hot water.

'He must be going to have a bath,' I said, 'we should go.'

'No, Henry uses his own bathroom, this is for us. Come on, aren't you going to strip off? I am.' She began to take off her clothes. Her red jumper, then her white skirt, without taking off the thin-strapped shoes, and, throwing the clothes on a chair, stood there, filling out a cream

31

slip.

'How do you know?'

'I know, she said. Out over her head the slip, out, off and down came the rest, stockings included, shoes stumbled aside, then, naked, she high-stepped into the bath. I stood, watching her. Breasts in real life turned out to be different from what I expected.

'Are you stripping off? Are you?'

'I won't,' I said, then more slowly heard myself repeating, 'I – won't.'

'Well, at least come over here, sit down and talk to me.' The chair by the bath had managed to catch a few of her flying clothes. 'So you like looking, do you?' she asked. 'Is that all you like doing? Is that all you are, a looker, a starer?' She wallowed, wiggling her shoulders down under the water.

'Why, what do you want?'

'Ah, what do you think I want? What are you, a child?'

'But, you – just did it, with Henry?'

'*But. But.* But is a goat.'

'But you did.'

'And what if I did?'

'Does he pay you?'

She threw a wad of soapsuds at me. 'He's a gentleman.'

'Oh, he's a gentleman, is he? A gentleman, is that what he is? And is your husband, what's his name, Jimmy? Is he a gentleman too? Or is a gentleman only someone with money?'

'Look,' she said. 'You think what you friggin' want, with your smart talk and your manners and . . . and your bank clerk's pasty face. I came from nothing. Henry

32

buys me clothes. And perfume. I meet people with him I'd never meet. Lifts me up in the world. That's why he's a gentleman. I never had a bath like this in my life till I met Henry. Henry says I'll have a fur coat one day. And anyway I'm not the only one, there's Madge too.'

'The housekeeper?'

'There's more to life than bank clerks, so there is. Henry's a kind man, to a lot of people.'

'Very – by the looks of things.'

I had turned down opportunities before, of course I had. Not as many as I pretended to, say, Affectionate Pat. The touching bothered me, the being touched, hand on my hand, skin on my skin. Kissing, curiously, could be all right, but I never understood touching and I knew that I had no understanding of it. Perhaps if I had some children – by some miraculous means – that would help; I could touch them, learn the process. Anyway, who wants intimacy? Did you have intimacy, my child? No, Father. Now there's a truth for you. No thank you, Father, no intimacy at all. Let them in and they'll hurt you, that's what I say. Oh, yes I liked the idea of it, I could kiss her neck or her knee as quick as the next man, no problem. Oh, yeah? Then why didn't I do it? There you are, boy, a naked woman for you, no holds barred. Sometimes I think I do not see what is happening in front of my eyes until it is much too late.

No talk for a few minutes, then 'Wash my back,' she said, and I said, 'Rose, that is about the oldest line in the business, I'll be waiting downstairs.'

I walked out of the bathroom, down the broad beaming staircase into the sunshine. I felt threatened and uneasy. The long-case clock struck again, six

33

o'clock, milking time, Rose still in the bath.

We drove to Bane in Henry's car, an American job, all
fins and chrome, immaculate, very long, chauffeured by
a man called Led. Henry did not introduce him, just
referred to him in an aside to me, 'He lost that eye in a
shooting accident. I wish he would wear a patch.' No
question of my taking my own car. Smooth as a
salesman, Henry ruled it out. 'You'll want to enjoy
yourself, have a few drinks, and if the evening gets too
long for you Led will run you back here. All right, Led?'
    Rose sat in the front. She, so far so garrulous, made no
attempt to speak to Led. Getting into the car she had
rubbed my left buttock and said, 'You'll give in. They all
do. I'll get you yet.'
    Henry turned to me and said very quietly, 'Led killed a
child, you know. One of his own children. A young boy.
Beat him to death. Got life. Came out after nine years.
Never mentions it. I agreed to go guarantor for him,
moral protector, overseer, sort of probation and guar-
dian. He mentioned the boy to me once, simply said, "But
he was a little rat", as if that justified it. Look at the size of
his hands. Look at them. He didn't use anything, a
weapon, that is. Just killed him with those hands, beat
him. Grisly business, it was.'
    The land through which we drove rose in sloping fields
from the cliffs, rich, good land, fertile, grain and dairy
farming, beef, fenced in by briar hedges or earthen banks
or barbed wire palings. Big farmers here – whose acres
have either been held for centuries, miraculously undis-
possessed in the Penal Days and Plantations, or in-

creased in the Land Division after the Revolution and the Treaty. Some got as much as a hundred acres, a ranch in their terms: we have their deeds and Land Certificates in the Bank. The next layer down were the smallholders who thinly improved their lots in the Land Division, tenants to freeholders. A third stratum came from nothing, had nothing, never would have: Rosaleen's people, never owning, never renting, people who lived on their wits and occasional employment. Unemployment money, doled out by the State, had only just begun. Those who took it lied their lives away, swore they never had jobs, never worked for anybody and dodged the inspectors sent in by the Department. Money from the State was free, in whatever form it came – grant, dole, pension. Some of them were even known to keep a dead parent's body from, say, the death on Monday and not declare it until the old age pension for that week had been collected on Thursday: true honourable Children (come to think of it) of the Revolution. They all mixed freely enough, the farmers, the cottiers, the smallholders, suspicious and litigious and secretive, but they depended upon each other for labour or hay or firewood, or meat when a pig was killed, or cheap milk.

'D'you read much, Mr Newman?' Henry asked.

'A lot.'

'The classics?'

'Everything, really.'

'And do you also write?' Measured questions. Should I avoid answering them?

'A little.'

'A little. A little what? A little poetry?'

'Yes, I suppose so.' I was hesitant.

'No need to be embarrassed, Mr Newman.' I had found a way: I would only tell him part of anything, not tell him for instance about trying to write more than a little poetry.

Henry was one of the two other strata which coloured in the rest of this cross-section. He belonged to the landed gentry, those of the old days, who had stayed, despite their religion, despite their knowing that no welcome existed for them, despite the fears they must have endured when, in the aftermath of the Treaty, the peasant victors with long memories burned down their houses and those of their grand neighbours. Easy enough for a few lads singing rebel ballads in a pub to set fire to a barn or a house on the way home and burn out some helpless, loftily-spoken old people, who sang their own anthems defiantly in the blazing ruins. 'Well that's the way it is,' or 'Sure, that's history for you' was the closest any expression came towards sympathy.

'Newman. Newman.' I thought Henry was addressing me.

'Newman.' He mused with my name. 'Nice. Mediaeval ring to it.'

The clergy completed the mixture, the priests, stateless and dark and powerful: bloodless in terms of class; their ordinations broke their social fetters. No matter how poor or doubtful his family, no matter how thick his accent, no matter how unprepossessing his origins, the ordained priest could enter any house and be assured of a welcome, fawning or fearful, but always courteous. (With one exception – illegitimate boys could never be ordained, just as paupers were denied Christian burial.) These men of the cloth ruled, feared as agents of greater temporal and spiritual powers, the representatives of the unexplained, they floated and strode untouchably through the people. They could – and had done and probably would again – bring down governments. They controlled all education, they managed the schools, they had the power to hire and fire the teachers, and they registered all births, marriages and deaths, their paper-work forming the human invoicing and receipting of the nation.

The road had begun to wind back out towards the sea again; a pair of trawlers followed the sunlight west. The evening mellowed into calm: the farms looked more peaceful than ever.

'What are our plans now?' said Henry. 'Are we going to have a good night of it, are we? Come on, Rose, what have you planned for us? Marvellous girl socially,' he added. 'Aren't you, Rose?'

'Aren't I what, Henry? I know I'm marvellous, but what am I marvellous at this time?'

'Marvellous socially, my dear Rosaleen.'

He turned to me again and said in a voice he did not care to keep down, 'You should have, you know,' nodding towards Rose, 'when you had the chance. A lot of men would have.'

'I thought a lot of men had,' I said. Did this man know everything? He laughed.

As the car slipped into the narrow rectangle of Bane Square, it struck me that the vehicle contained two men who had killed and a woman little better than a whore. Do not sigh, do not weep. Ah yes, the Risen People.

Henry spoke again. 'So, Rose, what are we doing, are we having a party?'

37

'A party for two, Henry.' She laughed.

'Now Rose. You know how old and infirm I am.'

'Not a bother on you, Henry.'

I asked, 'What are we doing, anyway?'

Rose said, 'Well, I have to stop at the Teacher's first. He has to fill in my form. So we might as well all call.'

'What's the form, Rose?' asked Henry.

'Good form, Henry.'

'Ah, Rose.'

'We're building an extension.'

'Won't he mind us all descending on him?' I enquired.

'Not at all. Eugene's an old friend of Henry's.'

'A very old friend,' said Henry. 'A very old friend. Of course he's much younger than me.'

'And anyway he keeps open house,' Rose said. 'Everybody'll be there.'

Henry turned to me again. 'Mr Newman, how are you going to vote next week?'

The country had been riven with a unique election campaign. The Government wished to change the electoral system from proportional representation to the straight vote. If successful they would stay in office more or less permanently, and to enhance the matter emotionally they had twinned the issue – which needed a referendum – with the emotive Presidential Election. All the people had to do was say 'Yes' to both the abolition and the assured re-election of the Government's great godfather, the Chief himself.

'I don't think I'll vote at all,' said Rose from the front seat. 'I don't know what's going on with that proportional thing.'

'Now, Rose,' said Henry. 'Women suffered to get the

vote. You must exercise the franchise. And you Mr Newman?' he insisted.

I certainly did not want Henry to know anything about my political views so I said that I had not quite thought the whole thing through.

'Sensible,' said Henry. 'These things do need careful thought.' I noticed that he did not volunteer his own preferences. 'And you can't be misled by the newspapers. You can't believe what you read in the papers, isn't that what they say?'

Rose chimed in, '"Look your loveliest with Knight's Castile" – that's all I ever bother reading in the papers.'

In this long open village with jostled architecture the Teacher's house ran back at depth from a shopfront behind a lopsided tree. The Teacher welcomed us.

'Such timing, Henry Mac, the man himself. I'm going off to play cards, you can come with me. And Rose. How are you, dear?' He put an arm around her waist and took her other hand as if to dance with her, a puffy man, a bit hail-fellow-well-met.

'The next dance is going to be a mortal sin. And who, may I ask, is this? Is this your young man, Rosaleen, your new flame, the passion of your heart?'

'This is Mr Newman. He's a singing bank clerk.'

'If music be the food of love. Well, you are all in time for a good evening. A little party. A few jokes, a bit of fun. All shades of opinion represented, as they say, roll up, roll up, a little sporting chance, and you, Rose, my love.'

He led us into a room, dark and old-fashioned plush. 'Come into my parlour said the spider to the fly. Rose, Rose, Rosaleen, am I the spider and you my fly?'

'There's nothing wrong with your fly as it is,' she said.

39

'Mr Newman, don't you admire Rose's very cheapness?' said Henry. 'So close to the bone of life.'

Led appeared, and at once the atmosphere changed.

'Henry, I told you before I never want to see that man,' the Teacher said, all ease gone from his voice, and he shouted the word 'man'.

'Led, you want to have a word with me? All right.' Henry moved lightly as a cat across the room, disappeared through the door, ushering the driver ahead of him, then a moment later returned.

'Now Eugene. That's all right, he's gone and he won't be coming back tonight. He will wait for us, but discreetly. Out of sight and therefore out of mind.'

The Teacher refused to be soothed.

'I told you before, Henry. Nowhere near here. Nowhere near me. Nowhere. At all. Understood?'

Silence.

Rose said, 'Where's everyone?'

The Teacher said, 'Teresa's away, I'm catering, I'll be back in a minute,' and when he went Henry said to me, 'Mr Newman, I do apologise. That little fracas was, I am afraid, because of my unthinking ways.'

'What was up with him?' Rose sat down on the big old couch.

'He taught the boy. The boy Led killed was one of his pupils, Led's young fellow. Eugene gave evidence. It was his evidence. Only his. No other evidence, actually, apart from the prosecution. And he lost on the double. A: he was distressed at the boy's death and the brutality of it. And B: when the case was over his neighbours cut him dead because he'd given evidence.'

I said, 'But surely he had a duty to give evidence?'

40

'This is a great place for silence, Mr Newman. You people from the west must surely know that. A great place for silence. No one speaks here, certainly not in evidence. Oh, it is all right now. When they eventually understood the full ramifications and the bad way the boy died they let Eugene off, so to speak. But they gave him the treatment for weeks. The silence.'

The Teacher came back bearing bottles. He poured for everyone. Except Henry. Occasionally I want to belong. Now I lowered my drink down the length of my throat and held out the glass humorously for more. The hit of the whiskey. There is a passage, a phrase in one of the verses. For there was lightning in my blood. My Dark Rosaleen. My own Rosaleen. Oh, there was lightning in my blood, Red lightning lightened through my blood, My Dark Rosaleen!

I should not drink. I should never drink whiskey. Certainly not in such gulps. Rose sat on the couch, skirt hiking. Domes, fat. And now I had seen, folds and creases and cones and shadow. Upon the ocean green. As I stood Henry said, 'Ah, Mr Newman, our new man, d'you like that, Eugene, our New Man is leaving us. Is that right, Mr Newman? Away to see your friend, your music man?'

'Yes, I must go.' Down the hatch, head back, glass emptied.

'Be sure to come back, Mr Newman,' said Henry.

The Teacher said, 'We won't be here, though, we'll be over at Connon's. We're not stopping here. D'you know where Connon's is? Show him, Rose.'

As I ducked my head beneath the low door and left the house, she got up and came to the street, pointing.

'Connon's is that pub over there. The one with the

41

shutters.'

'But that looks closed.'

' 'Tis. Closed completely. The daughters have it. The two of them. Wait 'till you see them. Jesus. Harpies. When the father died he left it in the will that they were never to open. Except the one day a year they have to – by law to hold on to the licence. Jesus, wait till you see them. One of them chain-smokes, a chest on her like the side of a church, lipstick tearing across the jaw on her. The other of them looks so like a man that she was the only woman ever to spend a night in Glenasmole Abbey, the monks never twigged.'

'How do I get in? If they're closed?'

'Oh, knock on the door, hard. I'll be listening out. Don't be long, will you? I don't want to be left alone too long with them shaggers,' and she nodded backwards.

The sea air and the noise of the waves cleared my eyes and my thoughts. I stood on the street. Then, as I walked in the dusk, something happened, and to this day I do not know whether I imagined it. An apparition came – surely my worried mind. A white shapeless phantom, large, like a very thin white sheet, seemed to advance towards me, quite quickly, flapping slightly, something from a bad old story, but weird nevertheless. It moved forward, clammy as if it would pass through me, like a soul. I turned, and it disappeared with increasing speed. Flapping thin and ghastly. No. Imagination, surely. Or – some kind of premonition.

The music man turned out to be not what I expected, but richly rewarding anyway. Opera, not jazz, he knew about. He played selections for me from piles and piles of records stacked up against the walls in his small, smelly room. He lay back, eyes closed, in a sloping mahogany chair, huge habitual stains on his trousers, his hands conducting in small patterns of gesture close to his body. He sat up from time to time. 'I heard her first in La Scala and I thought I'd die. I never heard such a magnificent voice' (he pronounced it 'vice'). Or 'You can always tell a black vice, be it a man or a woman. This vice made its debut (he pronounced it 'day-bue') in the Metropolitan Opera in nineteen hundred and thirty-one and he brought the house down, a rare thing for a black singer, can't you only imagine?' During one record, he took his spectacles off, committed a hand to his eyes and forehead and sat hunched forward. 'Not a chance. Not a chance in the wide earthly world we'll ever hear the likes of him again, and he singing like that since the year nineteen hundred and fourteen, made his debut in Donizetti, *La Gioconda*. The young fellows today may be good, but no, not a chance,' and a tear rolled down his face.

'Well, young Newman, I can't do anything for you if 'tis the jazz you're lookin' for, but I suppose you'll find somebody to help you. And you're a bank clerk. You ought to give that up and go into music proper, give yourself the silence or you'll never master a chord, a spell in jail, that's what all artists should have. Make a jail for yourself and put yourself in it. Or maybe you're in jail already, I don't know. Good luck now.'

I walked back along the street, past the small school and stood by the wall on the widened area which looked out over the sea. All quiet, clouds moving across the sky, stars, a moon due later. Should I go back to the group of people? No? Reasons fell short. I did not want to join them, but I had no choice, no car – mine was back at Henry's house, ten, twelve miles away. On the roadway, parked at the side, Led sat in Henry's car: would he drive me back? I moved towards him. He looked at me, shook his one-eyed head, and pointed me towards the closed pub door as if I should go in.

Rosaleen opened the door, humming.

'Come in, we're cycling into the drink.'

Obviously this part of the premises had never been used, not since the old man's death: chairs and benches were thrown up on tables and covered with old newspapers, while the brass rail above the frosted glass lower half of the window had not been polished for years. The high counter, even in this light of a dim bulb, had a thick skin of dust.

'We're only after arriving, we're in the back parlour.' We walked through – I had to stoop a little – into a kitchen. By a fire at the far end, under a dingy mantel and in a wide fireplace, sat two people – the famous sisters.

'Girls,' said Rosaleen, 'this is a friend of ours, Mr Newman,' and brought me across to shake hands with them. Their names were mentioned, but it would never matter, they seemed completely interchangeable. Two grotesques looked up at me, two large human frogs. One squat face drank from a mug, leaving her wide lipstick slapped along the side of it, another seemed in great danger of burning holes – as she had already done many times in the past – in the thighs of her antique jodhpurs. She went back to looking into the fire, aggressive and melancholy and dragging the last thin pinch out of a cigarette butt, talking to herself, and rocking a little on the rope seat of the chair.

'Take him in, we'll be in in a minute,' said one.

'In time for the cards,' said the other.

'You mean for the money, in time for the money?' said the first in a sudden burst, and laughed and laughed.

Through another door, into cigarette smoke, a large table, and with Henry and the Teacher, more strangers – a fat, wealthy-looking, youngish man with hair-oil, and a man in uniform, who had white hair and the weathered look of a hillsman.

'Mr Newman you have the good fortune to meet the pillars of our community this evening. This is Senator Rank, our representative in the Upper House. This is Mr Newman. He is a bank clerk and a singer. Rose calls him her singing bank clerk.'

I did not like being claimed by Rose but what could I say?

Then the man in uniform, who was introduced with great enthusiasm by Henry: 'And my friend Mercury who brings news from the gods? This is the most important man in our community, Mr Newman. This is the man who makes us face ourselves each day, whether we like it or not. Bills, cheques, threats. This is the man who brings us the truth every morning of our lives, who brings us to our senses and our senses to us. This is our Mercury, no wings on his heels I grant you, but on his bicycle, shall we say. This is our postman, Larry Dwyer.' Old joke: intoxicated by the exuberance of his verbosity. The Postman shook my hand.

Another voice boomed, the Teacher.

'Mr Newman had an appointment to see a man about some gramophone records. Was he all right, Mr

Newman?'

'All right, but it was opera, not jazz, he was interested in.'

'You'll get jazz here right enough, won't he, Rosaleen?' said the wheezy man, the young wealthy one.

'He will, Willie, he will,' she said.

'Ah, a man of the baroque, right here in Bane. Well, well, wonders will never cease. Of course there's no reason why we shouldn't have an interest in opera in Bane. Of course not.' Henry commanded this room, or certainly wished to.

'Our friend? Back from America? Danny, is it?' The Teacher looked not at me but at Henry. The Senator said, 'Far from opera he was reared.'

Henry said, 'Now, now, Willie, don't be a Philistine.'

'Was there any young fellows there?' said Rosaleen, and laughed. 'Isn't he a friend of Affectionate Pat?' and she laughed again.

'That will do, Rose,' said Henry. They cackled among their inferences, obviously they all knew the man I had been to see – 'the returned Yank' someone called him – and had put him down as doubtful in certain matters.

The Senator said, 'We'll start the cards.'

They had been having an argument in that room. I could tell. The air hung with it. All of them knew each other, and strain had come among them, I could feel it. Why didn't I go, leave, get out of there?

'I'm not much of a card player,' I said.

Henry replied, 'Well, sit and watch, Mr Newman. The talk will be good.' This table had been played on often: once it had been a good and expensive piece of furniture but, though much of the high polish remained, circles of stains and several burns had accumulated down the ages of card-players.

Rose caught my arm, breathing drink. 'Go and get the sisters,' she said, and turned with me. In a lower voice she added, 'You're not from here and you shouldn't be here. There's bad in here.' Searching their faces I knew what she meant. The Teacher had become too hearty, Rank, the young oily man, had aggression oozing from him, the Postman's complexion rose higher and he seemed to mutter. Henry was saying nothing.

I said to Rose, 'But Henry – he'll sort it out.'

'He won't. He can't. Go on. Go get the sisters.'

I did, I felt awkward, inviting those two into a room in their own home, but they were waiting and they followed me, a squat troop, grunting and muttering. A tray of thick-cut sandwiches had been placed on the table, and a further bottle of whiskey. Rose asked Senator Rank to put out his cigar – 'For a while anyway, the smoke.' The Teacher poured the whiskey, the Senator stacked the playing-cards. A chair was brought in, lifted over the others, settled into place. Around the table, in this order, sat Henry, myself – sitting back a little – the Senator, Rose – back, too – the Teacher, the two sisters – one sat right back, still smiling all the time – the Postman, who faced the Senator across the table. I could see every face.

The Postman said to me, 'Where are you from, Mr Newman? Aren't you the fellow staying over at Mrs Jordan's in Friarside?'

'This man knows everything,' said Henry. 'All our secrets.'

The Senator said to the Teacher, obviously picking up

an old thread of the conversation, 'If I was Eisenhower I'd want to stay in. They can't in America. 'Tis only eight years. Two terms of office. All those votes, wasted.'

Henry said, 'Mr Newman is from the West. Snipe country. Brown roads and black water.'

The Teacher said, 'Ike's had a good innings. I suppose Kennedy's just the right age for a President. Young enough to learn the job, old enough to know he has to.'

The Postman said, 'The Pope's older than Ike, and he functions.'

The Senator said, 'But not in all departments.'

A gale of laughter blew from the Teacher. 'No, indeed then, no. A truer word never spoken. Oh, damn good, damn good, Willie. Not in all departments.'

Senator Rank said, 'If Kennedy gets in, it'll be a great fillip to this country, a great fillip. Take us out of the doldrums, put us on the world stage. Success. Success.'

'We're getting bad enough as we are,' said the Postman. 'And we'll get above ourselves altogether if he gets in. The pass'll be rightly sold then.'

The Teacher said, 'What stage is he at now? Has he won the nomination?'

'God, no,' said the Senator. 'There's a year to go for that. He's only smelling out the ground now, feeling his way.'

Henry said, 'They have a complicated system over there, but it's very thorough.'

Senator Rank said, 'I'll be meeting him soon, maybe during the campaign if he gets that far. As an observer, and of course as a fellow in spirit. 'Twill be great to watch how they do it. Of course, they have big money in the game over there. Big support, in return for favours, of course.'

The Postman said, 'You see, 'tis starting already. We'll be having that style of wheeling and dealing here next. Then the money'll come and then the greed will start.'

The Teacher said, 'But won't Kennedy do us a power of good, all that style and show, and glamour and his grandfather emigrated from down the road. We should call a street after him, Kennedy Avenue or something, better than Gladstone Park or whatever.'

'Glamour my arse,' said the Postman, 'they'll all think here they have a licence to be American. The pass'll be sold.'

The Senator said, 'Rose, bring me luck. Pour more tea. And we'll start. The same stakes, lads? All right? Shove in closer, Rose.'

'No, I'm fine where I am.'

The Senator wheezed again, persisted, but sharper. 'Ah, come on, Rose, don't be a spoilsport. Sit here beside me.'

'Leave her alone,' said the Postman. 'She said she was fine where she was.'

The Senator hit his glass down on the table and said to the Postman, 'Look. Shut up.'

Henry at his most soothing said, 'Now, who's going to deal? Sit down Willie. Rosaleen, would you get us a new jug of water for the whiskey like a dear? Thanks very much. Senator, deal will you? Mr Newman are you in or out?'

I said, 'No, no, I'm out, I'll watch,' and I rose to get the water, at the same time as Rosaleen did. We bumped.

'Bring us two jugs,' said Henry. Outside, in the passageway, I said to Rosaleen, 'What's going on?'

'Oh, 'tis bad. The Postman had a go at Willie Rank before you got back. Rank had a fling with the Postman's wife or something – she's a lot younger – and the Postman knows some deal Rank is in on, and is throwing it up at him. 'Tis nasty, very. 'Tis the only time I've seen Henry rattled, you know how cushy he makes everything.'

'Why is he rattled?'

'I don't know. He must want something off Rank.'

'How well do you know Rank?'

'Mind your own business. Here. Give us a kiss.' She had my mouth before I could stop her, all across, wide and wet. 'Don't be pulling back, 'tis only a kiss, 'tisn't an accident, is it?'

I relaxed a little, but only to end it. Was this kind of predicament international? Could I find myself any-where in the world, in Czechoslovakia, or Finland, or Spain, caught like this – in a room with cunning and violent people? Could it be that I had only begun to wake up, to see the world as it was? Was it too late to run?

She asked, 'What are you doing afterwards, where are you staying?'

'I don't know. Henry's, I suppose.'

'Oh, good. Listen, though. This could turn bad.'

'How bad?'

'Awful bad.' Two jugs of water – my hand, I noticed, shook.

I had never seen a death. I had never even seen a body, laid out or accidental or anything. When my grandfather died I said I didn't want to see him and my aunt said, 'Fine. No bother.' And there are no murders here. One a year maybe, no more than that, a row in a kitchen or a pub or something.

As we came back into the room the Teacher said to Henry, 'And who will you be voting for, Henry? I suppose you won't tell us,' and laughed.

'Eugene, never discuss politics or religion,' replied Henry.

'Or the other thing,' said Rose.

'I wonder how we'll do at Ascot,' said the Teacher.

'I'd love to go there sometime,' said Rose, 'and wear a big hat.'

'With bananas on it,' said the Teacher and blew another laugh.

'So you're a man of the world, Mr Newman?' As he dealt the cards, the Senator spoke to me directly for the first time. Henry's phrase, and Henry replied for me.

'He is. He's musical, he has to be a man of the world.'

'Well, Mr Newman,' said Senator Rank, 'in some card schools they play for the clock, and that often means the clock on the Town Hall, so no damage done. Here we often play for money all right, but we often play for Rose too, all her contributions gratefully received and duly acknowledged. Isn't that right Rosaleen?'

'Ah, would you stop that,' said Rose, and some of the men laughed.

'Look – ' Rose began. The Senator put down his sandwich, rubbed his hands vigorously, said, 'Sit at the table anyway, Mr Newman,' turned to Rose, dropped a hand out of sight below the level of the table and said, 'Ah now, Rose, don't spoil the sport,' without any trace of a smile in his voice. She wriggled to the far side of her chair. The Senator said, 'All right, clear the table, open the cards, a straight and open game of poker, a good

51

clean fight and when I say "break", break and come out fighting and may the best man win, legs on her like a tractor and she'd plough for you.'

More laughter. The game began.

I remember every moment of that card game. With fear. I can still see the hands extending as they reached, the laying down of the cards on the table, the slowly growing unsteadiness as they drank – we were more than halfway down the second bottle of whiskey and one of the sisters had gone out for a third bottle – the way Henry looked at Rose trying to read signs or send messages, I could not be sure which, the fashion in which the Senator reached for Rose's hand from time to time, and never caring, a man sure of his ground, if he failed to reach it. I remember the face of the melancholy sister, brooding, disjointed, and the other one, slow-speaking and mannish and slapping her thighs, and swearing in words which were distorted to take the blasphemy out of them, made-up words, like 'Cripes' or 'James's Street'.

I drank – all the time. Oh, God. Henry chattered on, accelerating in his speech as the animosity between the Postman and Senator Rank grew. The Senator, as the night wore on, turned out to be even younger than he first seemed. Considering his fat bulk, when eventually he moved he did so with appalling speed and strength.

Shortly after midnight, Senator Rank said to me, 'What kind of music do you like anyway, Bank Clerk?'

Quickly, before Henry could do his speaking-for-me number, I said, 'Traditional singing.'

'Aha, the tenor with the n-yaaah in his voice,' said Senator Rank. 'One of them?'

'Yes. Sort of.'

'No "sort-of" or otherwise.' Inevitably, Henry spoke. 'He is not doing himself justice. Mr Newman has a most beautiful bass-baritone voice. A voice you'd love to hear, Willie.'

'Maybe I will, maybe I will,' said Senator Rank. 'What's your favourite song?'

'Actually you might know it. "My Dark Rosaleen".'

'Do not sigh do not weep,' said the Teacher.

'Know it?' said the Senator. 'Man dear, I was brought up on it.' He began to recite it.

'O my Dark Rosaleen,

Do not sigh do not weep.

The priests are on the ocean green,

They march along the deep.

There's wine from the Royal Pope.

Upon the ocean green.

And Spanish ale shall give you hope

My Dark Rosaleen.'

The Teacher said, 'By God, Willie, I taught you well.'

I asked the Senator, 'Are you a musician too?'

'No, boy. No. I'm a patriot. Don't you know your history?'

'How d'you mean?'

'Dark Rosaleen wasn't a woman at all. Well, she was but she wasn't. And haven't we our own Dark Rosaleen here.' He lunged again, towards Rose, who moved out of reach.

'I know that,' I said.

'Of course you do, and any right-thinking patriot should. Dark Rosaleen was the name for the whole country, her name hid patriots' aspirations.'

'And look what the patriots have done to her since,' said the Postman, very drunk.

'In the days before we had our freedom', the Senator continued, 'when our forefathers seemed to be singing a love song for some tragic lover they were actually singing rebel songs. That was Dark Rosaleen.'

'And haven't they hammered a fair job on her since?' said the Postman.

The Senator stared across at him. 'What's that you're saying?'

'Look at her now. Dark Rosaleen. That's what I'm saying.' He was immensely drunk. And angry.

'What's wrong with her?'

'Dark Rosaleen is right. Turned into a whore. Raped and drunk at the hands of the same patriots. The elected ones. The worst kind. And now Kennedy'll give them a bigger licence to cheat and fiddle. And we know who'll be in the van of that lot, who'll be organising the official reception for him. And picking up the receipts.' Even I knew he had gone too far, and I knew nothing of their arrangements, their codes. He could not stop.

'And look at what your crowd are doing in the Election.'

The Senator, in a voice as cold as stone, said, 'And what are they doing?'

'Trying to fool decent people. Trying to get them to say "Yes" when for their own good they should be saying "No". A cheat, that's what this bloody election is. A dirty cheat.'

The Senator, composed, said, 'It is a fair and legal election.'

'It is not. It's a bloody cheat. Dirt. If it was straight why

54

wasn't it written straight on the ballot paper. You're hoping they'll say "Yes" to the Chief and at the same time say "Yes" to the abolition of PR. Look at the way the ballot paper is rigged. Look at the words. "If you favour the abandonment of Proportional Representation put X before the word "Yes". That's crooked, that's what that is. Why doesn't the voting paper ask a straight question, a straight "Yes" or "No" – do you want to abolish PR? I know why – because your crowd would be in power forever, and what's more if I heard that you were the crook behind a lot of this, I wouldn't be one bit surprised. There isn't a woman or a girl safe from you.'

For the first time in my life I acted with some real resolve. I stood up and shouted, 'Stop. Stop.' No good, too late.

Silence. Like a blade. And then uproar. Shouted accusations. I stood, confused. The Senator scattered the cards. Then lunged. Scream. Shouts. He lurched and shoved around the table, pushing everybody aside in a dreadful urgency. His huge red fist balled, he hit the white-haired man. I do not know where the fist connected but I heard it twice, the squelch and thud all in one – huge blows. Who grunted – Rank or the Postman? I don't know. Directly behind the Postman's chair sat a large, black, shiny pot-bellied stove, black iron, unlit on this summer night. He fell backwards, to the sick sound of a crack.

2

The sun came out again a short time ago, and lit up the beach with a white light. Yet my body is cold. Fear. But I have suffered from fear since I can remember. Fear of failing, fear of falling, fear of dying. In the beginning it was fear of the dark, fear of my father's bulk, fear of the shapes in the fields, of the strong glances of strange people. A horse will throw you if he smells your fear; a dog will bite you. Yes, I gave off some trace, some spoor, some punished, victim's odour. Now, of course, I feel certain that this may also have singled me out – as well as my own stubbornness. This would account for the threat to castrate me. With the sickle. Funny – I didn't know I was stubborn, I'd always thought I slid around things, took the easy way out. There is no such thing as truth. There is no such thing as luck. I have to go over again and again the events as they happened, try to make some sense of them, of why it happened to *me*, how I got caught up in it, went along with it.

I could say that it began politically. This is not pretentious, or a pose; it really did. In this way. Remember the words of the Chief? I remember them, etched on my heart. '. . . a people who were satisfied with frugal comfort and devoted their leisure to the things of the spirit . . . countryside would be bright with cosy homesteads . . . fields and villages joyous with the sounds of industry . . . the romping of sturdy children, the contest of athletic youths and the laughter of comely maidens . . .'

Generosity. Decency. No crime. Everything accounted for. And a mood, to root it in. Heroism. Recent heroism. I still felt passionate about the Revolution. I read the fighting stories of each county and each city, each column and brigade of ambushing guerrillas. Much of it had taken place all around the fields of my childhood, and the memories, the legends, of those men, and their escapes and their adventures, all lived in real terms, down the road or across the fields. Night after night I heard the stories being told of huge and heroic deeds which had happened only ten years before my birth. My father, a self-appointed remembrancer, took down in a copybook the details of these heroes' experiences. They came to the house, silent, large men, with, as leggings, the sawn-off tops of wellington boots. I had a small wooden train, an engine, two carriages, red, blue and yellow, and I sat beneath the table, wearing a green knitted jumper with a cable stitch, by my father's legs, playing with this toy train.

My father's voice droned, asking questions, asking questions.

'What did you do then, Dinny?'

Silence.

'And what did you do then, Dinny? Did you run across the fields?'

'No.'

'What did you do?'

'I plugged him, sir.'

'Who?'

Silence.

'Who was it, Dinny?'

'There was one officer, sir. He had a revolver on a string around his neck.'

'That's a lanyard?'

'I think that's what it's called, sir.'

'And you shot him?'

'I plugged him, sir.'

'You shot him, Dinny?'

'I plugged him. Sir.'

All the big feet shifted, my father's polished brown brogue shoes, the men's big boots with their high, clay-streaked gaiters, all moved under the table.

'How did you get away afterwards?'

Another voice replies, more forthcoming.

'He was bleeding, Dan was, and I lifted him, half-lifted him, carried him, we went across the fields to Perdue's.'

'To Michael Perdue's house?'

'Yes, sir. And they tackled a pony and trap. We got a silent doctor who got the bullet out and got Dan back across the river.'

'"A silent doctor"? What was that?'

'One who wouldn't talk to the military, sir.'

'Where did you cross the river?'

'At the weir.'

'And where did you go then?'

'To Burke's of the Leinster.'

'The Leinster Farm?'

'Yes, sir. Over by the lake.'

Every name, every location, every family, every man – I knew them all. Their children sat near me at school, played in the yard, Perdues, and Burkes, and the doctor's son. My father said afterwards, when I asked him, 'Yes, they were brave men.'

My mother said, 'No, they were not. They never knew fear, and to be brave you have to know fear.'

My father said, 'Nevertheless they were the men who gave us our freedom.'

That is how my head filled up with ideals. These heroes now ruled our new nation, fearless men, and honourable, bred in the tradition of helping a bleeding friend across two miles of fields after an ambush.

So – essentially, then, I have always expected everybody to behave along the same lines of principle and integrity which I believed – which I was told – founded the State after the Revolution. Now I find myself sitting here in my car and I know I am probably in unspeakable danger. I believe that I must tell what I saw. They, the others, are intent on saying nothing, a cover-up. I will have to say what I witnessed. That is what I believe. They believe in silence, distortion, expediency, saving their own skins. Everybody except myself has told lies in this. They have hinted at a deal: if I join in with their story they will 'see me right'. Jesus – this is a hanging matter. Am I right? – to stick with those ideals which, after all, I was told, over and over and over again, 'founded the nation'? Or should I look after myself first? A new identity, eh? And forged so fast, within drunken seconds? No. Not at all.

When the Postman made that remark, 'Dark Rosaleen is right. Raped and drunk at the hands of the same patriots. The elected ones' I could feel the shock waves of the words. He had something on his mind, that man, something personal which was hurting him. Not the state of the country, nor the condition of drunken Rosaleen across the room. The remark was aimed at the Senator directly, like a thrown rock, or a punch. Rank felt the blow.

The Senator's hair is plastered down with hair-oil, his bulk, his blazer and tie, he fills the space around him. The Teacher places a hand on the Senator's arm, pointless, whatever the point. The sisters, fawning on Rank all evening, now shout, begin to bay. They stand up, and wave their arms. What do they look like? A pair of wild, stocky anthropoids, grunting and sinister. Rosaleen lurches across the picture, she too shouts. She stands, or tries to stand in front of the Postman, to get there she has to brush past the Teacher and the sisters, and drunk, she falls against their knees, against the table. 'Ah, Jesus, Jesus, ah, Jesus' she is moaning. The noise grows; the Senator shouts, 'Who are you getting at? Who do you mean? The elected ones? There's only one elected one here.'

The Postman has a silver harp on the lapel of his uniform, by a thin green piping of braid, and he has white hair, a jutting, reddening nose, weathered hillsman features, and he shouts, 'Your father died for this country, died for your famous Dark Rosaleen. He was shot on the side of a mountain, and look at what you're doing, you scut you. Cheating and stealing. That's all you are. A scut. A greedy, dirty scut. I see what you get in the post. I know what you're at. Grants . . . an' women – other men's women.'

Screams. Screams. Curses and screams.

Everybody moving, waving hands, pushing. Then the

noise of those blows, I hear it still.

Henry, though: I'll never forget how he sat. Like a cat, never moving, just observing. Saying nothing, just watching us all, and at that moment I understood what Henry did in his past – he spied.

The Postman looked frightened, knowing he had gone too far, but was too angry to stop. He shouted, 'You should be ashamed, you scut. Cheating. Interfering with decent people, interfering with decent women, cheating the voters.'

'Oh Jesus,' from Rosaleen, 'Oh Jesus, now 'tis all out, 'tis all out.'

'Shut up, you,' said the Senator to her. 'Shut up, you whore, or I'll shut you up.'

The Teacher, Eugene Scarry, let fly with a wasted and dreadful joviality, 'Lads, lads, can't we have a bit of peace? Come on, the game is more important than the row. Who's dealing? Come on, deal out the cards. Ah, lads.'

A momentary lull, not more than a second – though seeming longer – promised peace. Then the Postman shouted a third time, 'There isn't a woman in the county safe from you. You're a scut, that's what you are, Rank by name and rank by nature. A scut. Cashing in on your father's name to get yourself elected to the Senate. And to think our country is in the hands of scuts like you. Aah, Jesus.'

The sisters began in unison a chant – a whinnying, baying yell, 'Hit him, hit him, hit him. Hit him, Willie. Go on Willie, hit him.' I moved, despite my drunkenness, despite my fear, towards the door; the night air of the seaside town slapped my face. Too late, too late. It was all

61

over, wasn't it? Such confusion.

In a way that is the moment I remember most clearly. The noise followed me out. I stood in the doorway, one foot on the paving, wondering – should I call the police? No, these people settle their own differences. Run? But where? I had no car, I didn't know where Henry lived, I couldn't find my way back. Although I could have found a barn or a friendly house, I could have walked all night in this fine weather. To my right I heard the sound of footsteps: two men walked towards me, easily visible in the bright night sky, two big men. Ten yards away from me they too heard the noise, a short, hard scream which brought to an end the long roaring and shouting, though it can only have lasted less than a minute. Upon reflection, perhaps we heard the silence most of all.

The man on the inside, nearest the wall, stopped and then began to run. 'What?' he shouted at me, never finishing the sentence, and his companion started to run too. They came to the door, said to me, 'What was that? What was that?'

I think I said nothing. These men forced past me through the door. 'He's dead. He's dead. He's killed. You killed him.' Rosaleen's voice. Sound of a slap: you can always recognise a slap. A rising shriek as the slap landed, then a sobbing, much talk, the sound of Henry, then the Teacher, both saying, 'Oh, men, men, stand back, men, come away from him, Senator. Here, hold hard, let me through, stop, come back,' and the sisters' chorus saying, 'Good enough, fair enough, fair dues, he had it coming, that's the way, good enough, that's it, good enough, that's the way,' and a heavy coughing – Rank's.

I moved too, after the men, though I held back in the hall. 'Hallo, men, Bill, hallo, and Kit, is it? How are the two of you? Never better timed. Come in, come in.' The Senator had the smoothness of a gangster, an unstudied ease, a rural assurance.

Was I sober now?

'Senator, how are you? And Mr Scarry. Hallo Eugene, hallo girls. Rosaleen is it? Well now we're all here. Hallo Henry, how are you, girls? Who's that on the floor? Larry Dwyer, is it? Is he drunk, is he? 'Tis Larry Dwyer, the Postman. What is it, did you have a bit of an evening of it, itself?'

Henry came into his own, smooth and patrician. 'Well, gentlemen, never before have we so required the discreet assistance of the law. Is that not the case, Senator? Gentlemen we have had an unfortunate accident here, as you can see, and we may need some of your help; are you off-duty or are you on? You have no uniforms on.'

The remaining cigarette smoke swirled in the breeze of the open door. One of the sisters began to move the table back and the Postman, lying still at the base of the shiny pot-bellied stove, came into view, blood on his forehead, a hand slumped, splayed out.

'That man isn't drunk, he's hurt,' said one of the two new arrivals.

'That is correct,' said Henry. 'Which is why we need your help.'

Rosaleen had her arms folded tight underneath her breasts, as if she felt cold. I went forward, edging sideways between the two big policemen and knelt down beside the Postman. The blood came from a gash on the back of his head and spread fast out across his scalp, matting the white hair. I began to move him, to see his face and Henry said, 'Come away Mr Newman. Leave that man alone.' He said it so aggressively that I stood up at once.

'Get the doctor,' I said.

The Teacher said, 'Look, the man is hurt.'

'Shut up, Eugene,' said Henry, who moved into the middle of the room, cutting off my access to the fallen man. He said to me, 'You take Rosaleen out of here. Led will drive you to my house, where your car is. You're to stay the night there. Is that clear?' Led had appeared in the door. Henry took my arm as I said, 'No, I want to stay and make sure that man is looked after.'

Henry tightened the grip on my arm. 'We'll look after him,' he said, and the Senator said, 'We'll look after him,' and the sisters too said, 'Look after him, all right, look after him.'

I said, 'He needs a doctor. Get the doctor.'

Led, at a gesture from Henry, came forward and grasped my forearm, handed to him by Henry. 'Come on.'

'You too, Rosaleen,' said Henry.

'My bag, my bag.'

'Forget your bag. Go on, go,' the Senator shouted.

'No,' said Henry, 'she must find her bag.'

When she had found it, and her white coat, she ducked out along the dark passage to the door and climbed into the back seat of Henry's car. I turned to Rosaleen, 'What happened? Am I right? Did I see . . .'

She began, 'When Willie Rank stood up . . .'

Led, from the front seat, seen in the light of the

headlamps, said, 'Shut up.'

Rosaleen pouted, 'I will not. I have a perfect right to tell . . .'

'Shut – you – up.' Without turning his head, he reached a hand back, clenched his fingers around her right breast, wrenched and squeezed.

She screamed, 'Stoppit, stoppit, stop him.'

'Shut – your – mouth.'

I put my hand on his and managed to disengage it, firmly enough to convince him. I said to Rosaleen, 'We'll talk later, not now.'

Led said, 'You'll talk to no one. Do you hear. No one.'

I have never heard, I still have not heard, anywhere, at any time, such slithering, hard menace. We drove in silence through the darkness, her white skirt visible.

The night fields and their trees whipped past the car window. My head screams within. Tonight, this night, this Saturday night, I have seen this. A man dead? And if so, killed? Murdered? And what will now happen? Has he children? He has. And I? What shall I do? What are they doing back there? Covering up? What shall I do? Live up to my ideals? Of course. What else? First lessons in being a citizen, of the people, for the people.

Therefore – for once bring an ideal to meet a reality and speak out? I will, if I can. If it becomes necessary. Am I able to? My brain won't stop screaming.

When we arrived at the house I decided to ignore Henry's instruction. I would drive back to my digs in Craven, get out of here and fast.

I asked for my car and Led said, 'I put it away, in the garage. The boss said.'

And I said, 'May I have it please?'

And he said, 'The boss said you are not to leave.'

'But I want to go now.'

'You – are – to – stay. Here.' He switched off the engine and turned to look at me, one-eyed.

He opened the door and I walked gingerly past him. Madge the housekeeper who gave us lunch less than twelve hours earlier, said, 'This way, please, Mr Newman, Rosaleen,' and we walked behind her through the hall. She opened the door of a large lavatory hung with raincoats and said, 'Here, if you want to clean up. Your supper will be ready in a few minutes' – as if the hour stood at seven in the evening, not one in the morning.

I said to Rosaleen, 'I don't want to stay.'

'Why not? Henry'll not be home the night. He said.'

'He has fixed it all.'

She rebutted, 'Henry'll get us out of trouble. I told you, didn't I? Henry'd get Lucifer out of trouble.'

We went through the hall. 'Don't fall,' I said, which made her swear, though she knew how drunk she was. Outside in the darkness, I heard the car, I thought, drive away.

Everything is fixed. Henry has arranged everything. Being driven here, the meal, the silence from the housekeeper, the lavishness of the food and drink, the fire burning high in the grate of the long dining room, the feeling, deliberately generated, that it may only be early evening instead of morning's small hours. Henry must have telephoned while we were driving. And Madge, putty-faced and docile and completely in control of us, withdrawing as we reached coffee and brandy and a cigar for me and a silver cigarette box for Rosaleen, and Rosaleen not crying or even sniffling now, coming round a little and saying, 'This is the life.' A bloodstain on her white skirt. She must have knelt too, to touch the Postman. Can I cry? Can I weep? The priests are on the ocean green they march along the deep. Dark Bloody Rosaleen. And Affectionate Pat. Death in the air. Affectionate bloody Pat. Can I get out? Out of this bloody place? Why didn't I listen to myself this morning – here in this strange house?

Only one room was available upstairs. I tried the other doors on the landing, all locked, then I went back downstairs to sleep on a couch. Now, though, every downstairs door was locked too – the big leather chair beside the fireplace had been taken from the hall. Nowhere to sleep, except one room.

I went back, therefore, to the bedroom and through the arch into the bathroom I could hear her. She sang, she actually sang in the bath. 'She'll be wearing silk pyjamas when she comes. She'll be wearing silk pyjamas when she comes. She'll be wearing silk pyjamas, wearing silk pyjamas, she'll be wearing silk pyjamas when she comes.' That man is dead. I stood there, the bathroom door open, and now I appreciated that the bathroom formed part of Henry's suite. Twelve hours ago? Surely not? A lifetime, or more to the point a death-time, and the grue whistling upwards on the back of my neck. I undressed, except for my socks and underpants and got into the large bed, not much else to do. Beautiful suite of rooms, large sofa, fireplace, writing-table with leather racks of stationery, old mirror over the mantelpiece, another, a cheval glass, freestanding on the floor, dried flowers in great Chinese urns, an enormous bed. On the bedside table, with a marker in it, lay *Passage of Arms* by

Eric Ambler, Henry's bedside reading. It looked brand-new.

Through the door she comes, not a stitch, unabashed, rubbing herself merrily with a big cream towel.

'Are you a Catholic, Mr Newman?' She emphasised the 'Mr' with some relish.

'Used to be.'

'Used to be?'

'I'm a bit lapsed,' I said. Funny, I never used that word before now.

'Don't tell anybody that. They'd eat you around here if you said that.' A man is at least seriously injured, he may be dead, certainly his skull is bleeding and the people around here would eat me for lapsing.

'Are you a virgin, Mr Newman?'

'You're very formal.'

'You're – very – formal.' She mimicked, swinging the towel back behind her shoulders sawing it with both hands, jiving her body like a bulky dancer. 'I notice though that you didn't answer the question.'

'Well, what do you think?'

'I think you might be. I think you might be a virgin.'

'Wise or foolish?' With humour or jokes ward her off.

'Wise enough, or foolish enough.' She knelt one leg on the side of the bed and ran a hand along the sheet.

'Jesus, Henry's good to himself. That's linen, pure linen. He used to have silk though. I wonder is he coming down in the world? So you're a virgin. Well, well.'

She knelt on the bed fully, head and shoulders flung back. 'Do you remember your prayers, Mr Lapsed Newman? Did you ever hear this prayer?'

'O Holy Mary I believe

That without sin you did conceive
And now I pray while still believing
That I may sin without conceiving.'

'Didn't you ever hear that before? 'tis an old joke. You're an old joke if you ask me.' At which she burst out laughing and threw herself towards me to kiss me on the mouth. I ducked, tried to turn aside and her mouth caught my ear.

She said, 'Listen, don't you know about cuddling or anything? 'Tis only sport. C'mon, you'll enjoy it.'

Skin. Skin everywhere. I lay far away from her and through the night I winced, I stretched my body rigid. *From morning's dawn till e'en, You'll pray for me, my flower of flowers, My Dark Rosaleen! My Dark Rosaleen! You'll think of me through Daylight's hours, My virgin flower, my flower of flowers.* Love and death, is that it? – and that poor, bloodied man on that floor by the iron stove. She slept, as I woke and slept. After all the drinking she snored, so I knew when I could relax, otherwise if I slept while she woke she would almost certainly paw me. And so she did – or tried to. *Do not sigh, do not weep.* Oh, these people, those cards, this woman, the bloody land itself, the rotting ideals. *Would give me life and soul anew, A second life, a soul anew, My Dark Rosaleen.*

In the morning the door opened. Madge the house-keeper walked into the room followed by a girl I had not previously seen, a maid. Both women carried trays. Madge put her tray down on a table and opened the curtains, the light shone brilliantly. She looked us over without a hint of response, a look to ascertain facts.

'Mr Mac was here, and he's gone out again. Here is your breakfast. He says you're both to wait here for him but he doesn't know when he'll be back. It's half-past ten now and food will be at one.' She left the room, ushering the girl who had also taken stock of everything, a couple of witnesses, she and Madge, to the dishevelment, the bed smell and a bare-shouldered Rosaleen.

Rosaleen said, 'Madge is a cure. She'd cool Hell itself.' Then to me, 'How're you – virgin? I'll say this for you. You're the only man who ever –'

'Shut up, Rose.'

She rose, yawned, climbed out of the bed, and went to sit on the window seat. The light fell upon the freckles on her shoulders.

'What will you do now?'

'I don't know,' I said.

'What about Larry? That's what I mean.'

'I know. I was thinking. I bet that's why Henry is gone again.'

'Won't there be trouble?'

'I don't know.'

'If there is, though,' she said, 'Mr Henry Mac and Mr William Rank are the boys to fix it. They'll pay Larry hush money.'

'But he's dead, isn't he? He's dead. He was killed.'

'Ah, don't say that. Ah, Jesus, don't say that. He has young children.'

'He is dead, Rosaleen. That's why they got us out of the way. He's stone dead.'

'It was an accident. They'll say it was an accident.'

'It wasn't an accident. Rank hit him hard. Didn't he? You saw it. Knocked him back.'

'Larry was drunk.'

'That's not the point. He's dead.'

'They're awful powerful men' – by now she was whimpering.

'Who?'

'Rank. And Henry Mac.' She got up, her body heavier now in the morning sun, and whiter and younger and still shameless. 'Leave it to them. Get out. Leave it to them. They're powerful.'

'How well-known was Larry?'

'Ah, cop on, would you? Sure he's the Postman, he's about the best-known in the place. Everybody knew him. He saw them every day. He brought them their postal orders, their money from America, the forms for their grants. They liked him. We all knew he could be a bit bad-tempered at times, but he was the most popular man you could meet.'

'Was.'

She looked at me.

I said, 'You're saying "was". You know he's dead too.'

She wailed. Then, 'What will you do?'

I said, 'I don't know. I'll go downstairs now. My car is here, I'll see.'

'Henry told Madge we were to wait for him.'

'I might not.'

She started and grabbed my arm, 'Don't go, for Jesus sake, don't leave me – and don't cross Henry, he's worse than Rank, he has friends like you wouldn't believe. Whatever you do don't cross him.'

I said, 'I'll wait for a while downstairs.'

I did leave the house. Henry never re-appeared, nor Led. I found my Morris Minor in a stable, the key in the ignition and I simply got in and left. I did not know what to do or where to go.

71

About fifteen miles inland from Henry's house the road rises very steeply to a large and wide plateau, a lonely place called 'The Lakes', several of them. Their black surfaces are impenetrable, overlooked by the high limestone crags whose reflections, and those of the scudding clouds, gleam on the water when the light is right. Owls and hawks hunt here, grabbing mice and young rabbits up off the tufty moor. Nobody comes to the place much. Occasionally, courting couples park their cars, and sometimes in summer a local person will bring a visiting American cousin to admire the view, perhaps even take the long walk from one end to the other – it takes several hours. The sea can be seen clearly from the highest point and, east and west, far down by the coast, the toy clusters of Craven and Bane. One corner of these rocks has a freakish characteristic. For whatever reason, perhaps mineral, it contains – even generates – heat, pockets of great warmth, and it stays warm long after the sun has set – in which case the temptation to swim in the lake becomes misleading; the water will chill you to the joints.

I had to attend to so much now – the night that had just passed, the previous twenty-four hours and all the crudeness involved, the fright of events, the violence in the air, the unease of Henry's household, the genuine passions of those sisters, the annoyance and irritation which took me over when I thought of Rosaleen, and that red-faced man – he had a young wife, they said – that red-faced Postman with his white hair and blood, I saw blood on his head, on the collar of his shirt, and the silver harp badges on his lapels. Why did I not get out of it earlier? I know why – Rosaleen. When she got into the car I fancied her. I did. And then did nothing about it. Didn't think it through, didn't think as far as my own distaste. Typical – and doesn't it make me just as much of a hypocrite as the rest of them?

Aspens up here, and silver birch and arbutus. The shore of the first lake consists of rock peering up through the mosses and harsh grass. Murder? Will it come to that? If the man died surely questions will be asked? Murder? Or manslaughter, a worse word, a milder charge. I've never understood that: it still means a man slaughtered. Murder? Accessory before, during, after the fact? A murder charge? Unless they reported it to the police there and then, found him a doctor, took him to the hospital, informed his wife and family, got him a priest. Extreme Unction. The unction that is extreme. But of course all these things would be attended to. With a Senator there? And a Teacher? Relax. And, I forgot, God! I clean forgot – the two policemen. Yes, of course, of course, although I may have to give evidence – if there's an inquest, if he's dead. Evidence. Naturally. Anyone can have a row, or an accident. And how many other witnesses? Start with Rank, then Henry – don't trust Henry – and myself, that makes three, and one, four, and another, five, Rosaleen and Mr Scarry, and the two Connons, that makes seven, and the two policemen, if they count. Nine people altogether, nine witnesses in a small place. All of the same story. Could they cover up? That's what Rosaleen said: 'They'll cover it up.' No, they can't, they won't. Too many people. Rank hit him and he fell against the iron stove and he hit his head and fell on the floor. And Rank hit him hard. Into the face. They were baying, the sisters were baying – that's the word for it. Rank hit him and killed him. He called Rank 'a scut'. Let me get this right. If he hit him and killed him in a row it would be manslaughter. But if he hit him and killed him and then covered it up, would that make it murder? And I am a witness. Have I seen a murder? Oh, my God. Accessory after the fact. Before, during and after the fact.

I stopped in the middle of my stride, talking to myself. I could feel my face lifting towards the sky, as if it would give some balm, some healing. The lake stretched across from me, long and narrow and black. I stand on the rock, I see the lake, I see murder and all the implications, I walk on, I have time.

A gull, far from the sea, wheeled in over the water. Shadows lengthened and a breeze fluffed the foreshore. I shivered. I turned at the top of the long walk, back to the car by the other side of the lake, and sat in the warmth of those rocks, like a steam room or a warm laundry.

Nobody saw me there, only the sheep that mooched across the hill later, or a bird flapping homeward as darkness came. I fell asleep in the stone pocket. I slept for several hours, warm, cosy, I don't remember dreaming, and when I woke I was stiff – not too much, just enough to make me rise and shake myself. I walked down to the water's edge, threw a stone in. Why didn't I take urgent action? Why did I slip into lassitude? Why didn't I give myself the momentum to go to the police? I don't know. I just do not know.

When they asked me later to account for the hours I had spent after I left Rosaleen at Henry Mac's house they looked very sceptical. Well, for what it is worth now – it is true. I stayed by the black lakes most of Sunday until it became too hot and I drove away. I saw no living creatures except a hare, some sheep and the birds. I heard only the wind. Now, in the car, Sunday afternoon, I was hungry. I drove maybe twenty, thirty miles, saw a sign saying, 'Dinners and Meat Teas' and went in. I believe the woman later said that I 'looked wild', and that I 'seemed peculiar', that I was 'humming' to myself and 'waving back and forth in the chair'.

3

Long years on, in the crevices of the harbour town, late at night, when the lights still twinkle in the rain along the Causeway, when a door slams, when a car begins to make a noise in the street outside and is gone, when women walking homewards are heard rising and fading in conversation, when men will later mumble their ways from their kitchens to the pubs of the town, while their tongues suck the soda-bread crumbs from their teeth, the Postman's death will still hang there, like a little foul smoke, especially among those who know.

Silence. A minute's silence for the whole community. Silence corrupts and the disease spreads, children are born infected with it. Silence. Keep your mouth shut and your ears open. No one saw a thing.
   We. Saw. Nothing.

In the weeks that followed, Larry Dwyer's disappearance disfigured the town of Craven like a sore. Not so much the death as the subsequent failure to find out anything. Everybody stood accused by it, and the whole locality responded by withdrawing into sour gloom. A week after it happened a Dutch boat came in, always an event. It tied up at the West Quay, bringing a cargo of chocolate crumb for the creamery. A small clutch of feathered prostitutes sat waiting for it by the warehouses in the evening sunshine, but they were joyless, without

76

banter, and the sailors complained that these women wouldn't talk to them, and so the Dutchmen spent only a little money in the bars then slunk away. The following Sunday morning a man, an otherwise mild and peaceable man, a clerk in the Council, coming back from a walk along the Causeway, flogged his dog savagely in the square, reining the leash in tight and kicking the animal repeatedly. Another day the waves, in a flash tide, sucked and retched at the Causeway, tearing paving-stones away. Mercy of God, nobody was killed. For a long time things stayed as surly.

I came back to the digs late on the Sunday night, deliberately too late to meet anyone. At the Bank on Monday morning several large amounts of cash came in, weekend takings, I never lifted my head from my work until half-past eleven, when I had to go and post the ledgers. Later, when we were calling some of the balances against the passbooks which had to be sent out, the Agent, a spiky little man, observant, but I liked him, said to me, 'Are you all right, Newman?'

'I am, Agent.'

'You don't look it. Were you on the rant over the weekend?'

'Yes, Agent, sort of.'

'Were you at a party?'

'I was.'

'And did you sing, and how's the voice? My wife heard somebody saying the other day you were a star singer.'

'Oh, I don't know about that.'

We called off all the balances, I attended to one or two customers who needed change, we closed for lunch. Nicholas, the lanky porter, put the cashbox away with me in the treasury safe.

At half-past one the doors re-opened, and through them walked Henry Mac. He was wearing the same clothes – as if I mightn't recognise him. He came to the cash desk, greeted me as if he expected the deference due to a stranger, no camaraderie, and asked for change of a large note. As I counted out the smaller bills he said to me quietly, 'I take it you know the form.'

I said, 'What do you mean? What form?' My hands shook on the mahogany counter.

'You saw nothing.'

'But I did,' I said.

'You saw nothing,' he said again.

'But I did.'

He left, a finger on his lips, saying, 'Careful.'

The Agent came over to the cash desk. 'Who was that? Was that old Henry McCracken? That fellow has tons of money, rotten with it. Doesn't come in here with it though, has an account in the Royal Bank. Do you know him?'

'I've met him, Agent.'

'He's a useful contact. Cultivate him. He knows everyone. Funny that he was in here. Now he wasn't ever in here before, not in my time. Maybe he's checking us out. My wife said he was talking about me yesterday, making enquiries, to a friend of hers. Did he say anything to you about it now? I don't know the man at all. He'd be a nice coup for you Newman, if you got his account, he'd be worth a bonus to you.'

'He didn't say anything, Agent.'

Monday is always late, overtime. Late that night I ran into Rosaleen. She was waiting a little along the road from my digs. Jesus, the brooding I'd done. Should I go to the police? Did the police already know? Would it boil down to Henry's word and Rank's against mine? 'Leave it to Henry.' Something was up, that's for sure.

'I was waiting for you,' she said.

'Hallo.'

'Don't you know?'

'Know what?'

'Don't you know what's after happening?'

'No.'

'They buried the body. They buried Larry.' She started to cry, but maybe she was crying all along.

'Who did?'

'They did. Rank. And Henry. And Mr Scarry – Eugene. They buried Larry. And the Connons and the two cops. They buried him.'

Despite thick make-up a heavy bruise on her cheek shone.

'Where's your car? Can we go somewhere?'

'It's at the digs. Come on, I'll get it.'

'No. Pick me up. I'll walk on the road a bit.'

'Why?'

'I don't want to be seen with you. I'll tell you in a minute.'

We drove for about four miles to Flynn's Bridge. I turned off into a hilly wood, down a forestry road and into a quiet rutted avenue under the trees. She cried from the minute she climbed into the car, cried and cried, inconsolably. I said little to her: nothing to say. When we stopped I wound down the window, fresh air from the dusk, smell of hay and pine.

'This is terrible trouble,' she said. 'Terrible. And we're

79

right in the middle of it.' Funny: up until now I had scarcely taken account of the coarseness of her accent, of her skin.

'Awful. Awful. Awful. Christ.' More tears.

'What do you know? You said they buried him.'

'They did.'

'How do you know?'

'Willie Rank told me.'

'When?'

'He called out to the house. Today. I didn't go to work.'

'And what did he say?'

'He said he was trying to get in touch with you.'

'He knows where I work, I'm sure.'

'He didn't.'

'He must. Henry was into the bank today.'

'He does now.' She shook, rubbing her hands together all the time.

'What else did Rank say?'

'He said they buried Larry that night, Saturday.'

'But why did they do that?'

'They panicked, I suppose. Too much of the drink.'

'And what are they going to do now?'

'They're going to shut up about it.'

'They're not going to report it?'

'We're all to shut up.'

'Where did they bury him?'

'I don't know. He said they put his body and his bike into the back of a car and drove out towards Dunstown, out towards where the old mines are.'

'The old tin mines? Where the chimneys are, the shafts?'

'Yes.'

'But a mineshaft can be searched.'

'There's roadworks, too, a big new road out there. That's what I think.'

'Why do you say that?'

'He let slip something about tar. And his arms still had tar on them. He asked me for butter to take it off.'

She cried again, wailing this time. I took her hand.

'What is it? What is it?'

'When he came to the house he told me that no matter what anybody asked me I was to shut up, say I didn't know a thing. And he grabbed me and hit me. And – did me.'

'"Did" you? What do you mean?'

'Did me. Yes. I'm all bruised. I know you don't think . . .'

'Hold on. What do you mean – "did" you?'

'You know – did me. You know.'

'You mean – he forced you. Raped you. Is that it?'

'You think that it mightn't be force, that I'm easy meat. But it was force. And he hit me. Here.' She showed her face. 'And here.' She unbuttoned her blouse and showed me marks beneath her neck. '"That's a warning," he said, and here.' She lifted one breast, the right one, nearest me, and underneath glared three ridges of weals, traces of blood on them. 'His fingernails. The same on my behind.'

'Have you told the police?'

'Are you mad? He owns half of them.'

'Come on. The police are safe.'

'I'm not. He'd kill me. Or he'd get somebody to.'

'Is that what you're frightened of?'

'I'm caught anyway,' she said. 'If I tell the police Rank

will kill me, sooner or later, and if I don't tell them and they find out, murder is a hanging matter. What he's banking on is them never finding out. He says if there's no body they can prove no murder.'

'But you can tell them where the body is buried,' I shouted.

'I'll never do that. Never. My life wouldn't be my own around here. I'd be an informer. For the rest of my life. They'd boycott me.'

Hail the Risen People. I remembered the story of the Teacher. He gave evidence in Led's son's murder. Ostracised.

'By Jesus, I'll tell them,' I said.

'Oh, don't, don't. You'll get me killed. Don't involve me. They'll know where the story came from.'

'Hang on till I get this straight. Rank came to your house, told you they had buried the Postman's body – you think it was either down a mineshaft out at Dunstown, or under the tar in the new roadworks – then he raped you, and hit you so that you would be frightened, having given you just enough information to involve you on the same level as himself, so that if the information got out he would know where it came from? And above all he thinks they will get away with it because nobody will say anything and there's no body?'

'Yes. He said they left the bicycle at the edge of a quarry cliff down to the sea to give the impression Larry might have fallen off the bike. The Teacher is going to say Larry was very drunk.'

'Do the police know?'

'Larry's wife reported him missing. Rank was out there while the children were at school.'

'So he – "did" – her too?'

'I don't know. I doubt it. They say he's at her a bit anyway. Some of the reason Larry was having a go at him is because the lads at the post office were jeering Larry because his wife was an old man's darling – she's several years younger than Larry, though he was a very good-looking man in his own day – and that an old man's darling is a young man's fancy and that Willie Rank was the young man. I saw them dancin' where they weren't supposed to be, over in Ross at a farmers' dance where they're hardly known. So he said he called casually and then told her he'd help her to find Larry.'

I got out of the car and stretched. Beautiful night, a calm night, the sound of the surf in the distance. Rosaleen got out of the car too, and walked across the springy grass towards me. I sat down, she stood above me. 'We could run,' I said.

'Aw, where? Have sense.' She sat down.

After a while she said, 'Give us a hug anyway. No harm intended.'

In the hallway of the digs the landlady had left a note. 'A man came to see you. He didn't leave a message. Wanted to know what time you were going to work in the morning.'

Tuesday the 16th, even now, seems like the longest day of my life. Every time the bank door opened I jumped.

'You don't look too well, Newman.'

'No, I'm all right, Agent, I have a bit of a chill, that's all.'

'Nothing bothering you, is there? No woman trouble, heh?'

'No, no.'

The door closed at three o'clock and luckily mountains of work had to be done, a ledger balance, always troublesome. The half-year arrived in a fortnight, everything had to be shipshape, all foreign exchange returns had to be completed, we had stacks of dollars which had to be remitted to Head Office so that the half-yearly Branch Return could be completed when the General Ledger had been closed off and balanced. No problem staying until half past seven and the walk home would take half an hour.

Two things happened. As I left the bank and tested the alarm key a voice called.

'Hah, young Newman. How's the form?' Affectionate Pat, from the front door of The Enterprise.

I walked over.

'Eh-heh, you're looking a bit pale about the gills. What are you up to at all?'

'Nothing, Pat. Working too hard.'

'And drinking too little. Are you coming in?'

'I'm not, Pat. I have no money.'

'Ah sure the name is good, the name is good, money in the bank. Listen here to me now. They tell me you met the going concern.'

'The what?'

'The Rose herself. Dark Rosaleen. The going concern. The town bike.'

'Pat, I'm ashamed of you.' How did he know? How did he know?

'Listen here to me. I want you to come in tomorrow night without fail.'

'For what, Pat?'

'There's somebody I want you to meet. To your

advantage as they say. Around half-past eight, right?'

'I might, Pat.'

'No "might" about it. You will, won't you?'

'All right.' I moved away. It might all have eased by then.

'That's terrible about Larry Dwyer,' Pat called after me.

'About who?'

'Larry Dwyer. The postman.'

'What happened to him?' Oh, God, I'm into it now. He'll give evidence that I 'denied all knowledge'.

'They don't know. He's gone missing. People are upset. Very popular man. Very popular. I hope there's no foul play. See you tomorrow night now, right?'

'Right, Pat.'

Directly over the Causeway my habitual route homewards turns sharp left into a stretch of road overhung by trees, no houses for a hundred yards or so, a quiet road. A car drew up beside me and a voice said, 'Hallo, Bank Clerk.'

Two men got out, strangers, well-dressed, big. A third whom I could not see – they obscured my view of him – stayed in the car. The men began to speak.

'Listen, Bank Clerk, you saw nothing,' said the first.

'Nothing whatsoever,' said the second.

'You know nothing.'

'You heard nothing.'

'Not a thing,' said the first.

'Not a single thing,' said the second.

From behind his back the larger of the two brought forth a sickle.

'Do you know what this is?' He held it in front of my

face. ''Tis a billhook, that's what it is.'

The voice from the car, Senator Willie Rank's, said, 'You left Connon's around midnight. You took a lift home with Henry Mac because your car was at his house. By the time you were leaving, Larry Dwyer was blind drunk and you weren't much better yourself. People were offering him a lift home and he was refusing, saying he would cycle, that he was independent. Everybody told him, including yourself, not to be foolish, but he wouldn't listen. When you got to Henry Mac's you were too drunk to drive, Henry wouldn't give you the keys and you went to sleep in his house. As we all know, Bank Clerk.'

At which point the man behind me pinned back my arms and kicked my legs apart. The one in front bent down, placed the point of the sickle in my fork, just at the point where the cleft of my buttocks ends and my testicles begin, the tender fulcrum part of the entire body, directly underneath me, and pressed – not quite hard enough to tear the fabric of the trousers.

He repeated Rank's last words up into my face, 'As we all know. Bank Clerk.'

When they had gone, and I got to my digs, I vomited. And vomited. Not a wink of sleep did I get that night. Finally I got up, dressed and drove, at five in the morning, to the village of Bane. I parked the car down a lane and walked into the village. In this early light Connon's pub looked derelict. Every bone of my body shivered. I turned towards the sea and walked from the square down the long – the only – street in the place, where the phantom had flapped by, then past the Teacher's house and along to where the road finally left the village, winding off between high banks of sea-grass and dunes. The sea hardly breathed. Wasteland. Place of skulls. As I turned back and faced the Teacher's house I saw someone at an upstairs window. He must have seen me too. Good, I needed somebody to talk to, and he couldn't sleep either. I waved, the face disappeared and as I walked towards the house the door opened. The Teacher said, 'Get out of here, go on, get out. Out, you'll get us all into trouble, out, out,' and closed the door. I leaned against the postbox in front of his shopfront not knowing what to think. Then I turned and went back to the car.

I drove along the Dunstown road with no idea of what I was looking for. I knew where the mineshafts were – the old chimneys could be seen from the road and from the beach. The nearest one stood five hundred yards up a hill, through gorse, over rough ground. No trace could be seen of flattened grasses, of a heavy load having been dragged. The weather had been calm, the grasses would have remained flat. In all I wandered around four of the mineshafts. These remote places receive few visitors, and nowhere did I see anything to suggest that anyone coming to this spot had carried or dragged something heavy.

Further on, down where the road winds by the shore, the roadworks contained huge idle machinery awaiting the day. Great trenches, hundreds of yards long, several yards wide, had been dug and large barrels of tar, perhaps a dozen or more, stood by the roadside. I walked forward to the place where the roadworks had most recently been completed. Any object laid under the foundation, then covered with a foot of tar, would never be found again. As I left a car coming towards me stopped, then, as if it had seen me, turned on the road and drove quickly back the way it had come.

The sun had risen fully, little lemon clouds already. It was going to be a lovely day.

4

Statement of Patrick Newman

I, Patrick Newman, aged 29, a bank official, of no permanent abode, but temporarily residing at Bayview, Friarstown, Craven, have been charged with the murder of a postman called Larry Dwyer. I did not do it. I may have been one of the last people to see Larry Dwyer alive but I had nothing to do with his death. Last Saturday morning, while travelling in my car to see a music teacher in Bane, I gave a lift to a woman standing by the roadside. Her name was Mrs Rosaleen Mara or O'Mara. After travelling a short distance she asked me to stop and give another lift, this time to an elderly, well-dressed man, who was introduced to me as Henry Mac. He invited us to his house for dinner – lunch, he called it – and we stayed there for quite some time, had a meal, and the woman and I had some drink. Late in the afternoon we motored, all three, to Bane in a car driven by an employee of Henry Mac. We called to the house of a Mr Eugene Scarry, a teacher, because Rosaleen O'Mara said he was filling in some forms for her. From there I went to keep my appointment with Mr Daniel Roach, a retired music teacher in the same village. As I left I was informed that I should return, not to Mr Scarry's house, but to another building, a 'closed pub' belonging to two sisters, the Connons, whose place was pointed out to me. When I had finished my appointment about two and half hours later I went to the pub and was admitted to the parlour where a card game was about to begin. The other participants and people in the room, other than those I had met that day, were previously unknown to me, but I believe they were Senator William Rank, the Connon sisters and a Postman named Larry Dwyer.

Much drink was flowing and there seemed to be a needle between Senator Rank and the Postman. Several arguments were on the point of breaking out and only the intervention of Henry Mac and the teacher Mr Scarry prevented the two men from coming to blows. Finally the Postman made some remarks which particularly angered the Senator. I do not recall the precise words, as they were half-shouted, but they were something like 'Raped and drunk at the hands of patriots, elected ones'. The Postman made further derogatory remarks about Senator Rank and called him 'a dirty, greedy scut'. I took it to be a severe criticism by the Postman of Senator Rank's morals. The two men stood up and began shouting at each other. My view was obscured by Rosaleen O'Mara who tried to reach across the table and come between the two men. I then heard two blows landing, saw that Senator Rank had hit the Postman who then fell. He definitely hit him. As the Postman landed there was a crack, as if he had hit his head on the black iron range or stove which was behind him. There was no fire lighting in it. He lay still on the floor partially under the table. I left the room, not wishing to be part of anything. Also I was shocked, and had had too much to drink. As I opened the front door two men – called, it turned out, Bill and Kit – were walking past the house along the pavement, and I told them something terrible had happened. They came in and were greeted by Henry Mac and the others whom they knew and it became clear that they were local policemen. I went to attend to the postman who was still lying on the floor, but was told to keep away, although I got close enough to see that there was profuse blood on his collar and hair. I was then told by Henry Mac to leave the room and that the car would take me and Rosaleen O'Mara back to his house where we were to stay until he came back. I went in the car and stayed the night in his house, and left the following day. I drove up to the Lakes where I spent all Sunday and came back to my digs on Sunday night, then to work in the bank on Monday morning at 9.20. I had nothing to do with the death of Larry Dwyer other than that I was there at the time, but I did not kill him or touch him. He seemed a nice man to me, and I will swear on oath that I had nothing to do with his death.

Signed: Patrick J. Newman, 17th June 1959.

The 17th of June was my father's birthday, sixty-five, retiring age, although he may get an extension until sixty-eight. I didn't send him a card. So Affectionate Pat is in on it, is he?

'Who're you voting for?' he had asked.

'Pat, I'll not bother,' I had said, 'they're all tarred with the same brush.'

Then he directed a remark past my shoulder, 'I think Sergeant,' – I was sitting up at the counter with a small whiskey – 'this might be the man you're looking for.' And the hand on my shoulder. So this was the 'someone' he wanted me to meet, to my 'advantage'. The treacherous, bald shark.

Enter a detective. With red hair. 'Will be taken down and may be used in evidence against you.' Why do they call it 'cautioning'? It made me want to throw caution to the winds. To my 'advantage' I made a statement at about nine p.m. As they took me to the police cells they told me not to be worried, that very shortly I would have company. Not much room here for company, one other cell. At half-past eleven, when I was thinking about sleep, not much chance though, a curious thing happened. The door leading to the cells opened and the detective who arrested me, a flat, ordinary man, stood in the doorway, holding it open so that I could see past the filing cabinets into the office outside. First of all, I recognised the Agent from the Bank, deep in conversation with somebody at the desk. Then, on the far side, I could see commotion developing, as a large group of people came in from the street, and I recognised them too; Henry Mac, Senator Rank, the two Connon sisters, the Teacher, Eugene Scarry. What a round-up. The red-haired man closed the door again, and it seemed he merely wanted me to see what was going on. He has arrested all those people? And he wants me to know? Is he on my side?

A quarter of an hour later the door opened again, and the Agent came in accompanied by a uniformed policeman. The Agent stood outside the cell – though they opened it for him – and spoke to me. I had never seen him in a cardigan before.

'Newman, are you all right?'

'Yes, Agent.'

'What's going on here at all? I was out at the Bridge Club and Eleanor came over for me.' Eleanor was our sole lady clerk.

'I've made a statement.'

'I know. They're going to let me see it. Is there anything you want?'

'To get out of here.'

'You'll have to wait a while for that I think. Anything else?'

'No. Except –'

'Except what?'

'Don't tell my people. If anyone is looking for me. Tell them I'm out sick or something.'

'Look, it'll be in all the papers tomorrow. This is the first murder' – he changed tack – 'this is the first thing like this to happen here, or anywhere for a long time. Everybody is talking about it, he was a well-liked man. Are you sure you're all right?'

'Yes, thank you, Agent.'

'Listen, I have to ask you for your keys. To open the safe.'

'They have them. In the office outside.'

'Of course. You were searched.'

'Yes. What's the position about that?'

'About what? The job and that?'

'Yes, Agent.'

'Well, I suppose you still have your job, although until all this is settled they'll hardly let you back here, into our office. I'll get on to Head Office in the morning, I'll have to before the court opens, there's a hearing first thing.'

'A hearing?'

'Yes. Charges, a whole lot of them.'

'A whole lot?'

'Yes. Not just you. They arrested several people on the basis of your statement. I don't exactly know how many. You'll all be in the court first thing.'

'Is that good or bad?'

'Well, it'll bring it all out in the open.'

'Should I be worried, Agent?'

'Well, it's not pleasant at all, but if you're telling the truth and if you hold on to yourself I suppose you'll be all right.'

'How about clothes and things? Have you any soap, a clean towel or anything?'

'I'm all right for the minute.'

'Look after yourself. My wife sends her best wishes. Here's a paper for you, in case you didn't get time to see it today.'

Police on point duty took off their tunics in the heatwave. Dutch difficulties in New Guinea. Some parts of the country, though, will have light scattered showers, westerly winds. 'Fieldman – If You Watch Today: The deep dark green of the pastures and meadows is tinted with browns and purples where the flowerheads of the grasses are ripening. Tall thick thistles stand up like four-foot torches. Orchid after orchid appears, deep amongst the grasses . . .'

I am in jail, probably to be tried for murder, maybe to be hanged.

When he had gone Henry Mac and Eugene Scarry were led through the door and put in the next cell. Both men looked at me. Neither spoke. The Teacher appeared embarrassed and angry, Henry Mac gave me a look I could not fathom, long and clear and cold, with no expression. Although my cell had an extra bed pallet in it, I spent the night alone. The two men in the next cell spent a long time in quiet conversation. I could not catch a word. I never attempted to speak to them.

The breakfast tasted better than I thought it would, although there was no chance to shave. Then we walked across an alleyway in the bright sunlight, hidden from the street by a high wooden door, into the courthouse, next to the police station, and after half an hour in a corridor – I was kept separate from the others – we were brought up the steps into the dock. Everybody who had been there on that night had been arrested, including the Senator, the Connon sisters, Rosaleen and the two policemen who arrived on the scene, and Henry Mac, the Teacher and myself, nine of us all told, stood in the dock, which extended into a part of the seating which they had railed off. The court had filled to bursting with people and they made a tremendous commotion, completely unexpected; I did not know how to react. I kept my head down a little and only raised it when I could look straight ahead. I looked at Rosaleen first. Her face had another bruise on it, a bad one this time, and her eye had been partially blackened; both her eyes were swollen from crying. She glanced up, saw me and looked down again without any communication. The Senator and Henry Mac seemed completely at ease, no problems. The two sisters looked more than ever like creatures out of a prehistoric comic book, wild and unkempt, though the lipsticked one of them had dressed more smartly than the other. The greatest shock came when I looked at the two policemen, whom I had only seen briefly and not very clearly. They both had the appearance of men who had come through a bad brawl. One was even still bleeding slightly from a cut lip, both had blackened eyes, injuries more recent than Rosaleen's black eye, and one had an enormous reaming on his forehead.

The hearing, in front of a district court judge, was short. Each person was formally charged 'that on the night of Saturday 13th June 1959, or the early hours of Sunday, 14th June 1959, you did unlawfully take the life of Laurence O'Dwyer, a postman of Uaig, Craven, and did thereafter conspire to dispose of his body in a manner designed to thwart the course of justice.' Only three people had legal representation, Henry Mac, the Senator and the Teacher, and their lawyers applied for bail, which was refused. The court adjourned for seven days in order to allow all of us to be represented. We were then taken away, the men to Grant Prison, the women I know not where. Curiously I travelled alone, in a police car, though I saw the other men being escorted to a van. Nor did I see any of them in prison. Once I saw Henry in the distance across a railed-off corridor, looking well: we all had permission to wear our own clothes. I was still in the charcoal grey suit I wore to work. But I had no contact whatsoever with the others.

I had three visitors – the Agent, the detective who arrested me, and my State-appointed lawyer. The Agent brought a letter from my father – sent care of the bank – which began, 'Dear Patrick, Well, I must say this is a nice retirement present for me and your poor mother . . .' I read little more of it, just enough to glean that they would not be visiting me. The Agent said that my father had telephoned, but really to ask the likely extent of the publicity, 'whether there would be much more in the papers'.

'What did you say to him, Agent?'

'Well, I didn't know what to say, so I suggested to him that we should all be supporting you now. In your hour of need.'

'What did he say to that?'

'Well, he didn't say anything. Is he a very cold man, your father?'

I did not reply.

'I gathered that. Oh, and I met that barman from The Enterprise, the one you call Affectionate Pat. I gave him a flea in his ear, I can tell you.'

'How's that?'

'For the way he was talking.'

'What was he saying, Agent?'

'Oh, it doesn't matter, but he's in cahoots I would say with some of the others.'

'Why do you think that?'

'To be blunt, he was trying to say to me that they'll all get off.'

'And that I won't?'

'More or less.'

'That they'll throw the blame on to me?'

'More or less. That's the talk they're putting out.' He fidgeted. 'You don't smoke, do you? I brought you cigarettes just in case. Would you like a few chocolates instead? Oh, by the way I spoke to Head Office. They're puzzled, like we all are, but they're not unsympathetic. They're sending down a relief cashier, an inspector or a bank legal man might come too, and what they're doing is paying you, the full salary, until all this boils over one way or the other.' He caught himself repeating the

phrase, 'One way or the other' and became embarrassed.
'My wife sends you her regards. I'll try and get to see you
at the court on Friday. Look after yourself. Oh, I brought
you the papers. Do you think you want to see them? It
might be no harm to see what they're writing about you.'

Front-page news. The newspapers, several days of
them, national and local, had huge stories, interviews
with the dead man's wife, showing her and the children
forlorn outside their cottage. The wife seemed very much
younger, the children small, winsome. Most surprising of
all, the papers carried reports of the agitation in the
streets outside the courthouse after our hearing had
ended. Two themes came across, that the two policemen
had been assaulted in custody and that otherwise decent
people, namely Henry Mac, the Teacher and above all
the Senator had been refused bail. The common refrain
seemed to be that there was no evidence of any
description upon which these people should have been
arrested, no proof of any kind that a murder had been
committed. It looked as if they hadn't got hold of my
statement: and of myself, little had been written, they
had no photograph, a reporter had traced my home
address, but found nobody in the house when he called.
They had spoken to the Agent, who had no comment
other than that I had been a reliable and satisfactory
official and a congenial, hard-working companion during the year or so I had been in his branch. An inside
page carried a small story with nothing to it, called 'The
Singing Bank Clerk'. Nothing to it at all, except for one
inaccuracy, an invention, which made my heart jump.
'A colleague who did not wish to be named spoke of
Newman's ferocious temper, uncontrollable, especially

after a few drinks.' My head screamed, 'Not true.' What was it the Agent had said – 'More or less' – when I asked whether they would try to throw the blame on me? That piece was planted. By Rank. Or Henry. 'A colleague . . .' – impossible to check.

My next visitor, the detective who arrested me, a Sergeant Luke Nagle, sat in the cell with me, a quiet man, businesslike, clear in his mind.

'Have you anything to add to your statement?'

'No. Not a thing.'

'Did you meet any of the accused since Saturday night? I mean before you were all arrested?' Trick question. I did meet Rosaleen, but if I say that she will be in danger from Rank and his friends. And even though I was threatened by his men I did not actually see Rank, just heard what I thought was his voice.

'Look,' I said, as if I hadn't heard the question, as if it were irrelevant, 'I'm anxious to help all I can, but I don't know where I'm going until I get some advice.'

'Why didn't you report it in the first place?'

'Because.'

'Because what?'

'Because – I don't know. Because I was confused. I didn't know they wouldn't do something, look after the man. You know, report it, get a doctor, or get him into hospital.'

'Fair enough,' he said. 'I see.' Are they believing me? 'If you want to talk any more tell the warder and he'll get hold of me.'

My lawyer, Mr Hennessy, turned out to be foul-mouthed and philosophical. When I asked him – much later – why he swore so frequently he said he had to, he felt so disgusted with himself so often. He said he supposed I didn't do it, didn't kill the man, and I said I didn't, that I was there when it happened, witnessed it, could describe it in detail, had already done so in a statement. He said he had seen that and normally he would wish that his clients didn't make statements until he was there but this was such a clear statement he didn't mind, and in any case he didn't know I was going to be his client. 'People shouldn't make statements anyway. They should shut up.' I asked him how serious the entire matter was and he said he thought it was 'tricky enough', but that the truth comes out in these things.

I said, 'But they're trying to say he disappeared.'

'They are. They are.'

'Dangerous for me, then?' I asked.

'Dangerous. Do you know that already?'

I told him about the incident with the sickle, and Rank in the car.

'Yes,' he said, over the top of his glasses. 'And I know the thugs who were with him too. Why didn't you put that bit about the billhook in your statement?'

'I was afraid. And besides, I wanted to keep it for later.'

'To see how the land was lying?'

'Sort of.'

'In case the police were going to be paid off?'

'That sort of thing.'

'You're not as green as you're cabbage-looking. Have you looked at what's against you?'

'You mean the charge?'

'No. The people. At who's against you.'

'Not in detail.'

'Right, I'll do it for you. Take the two policemen. Forget them. Not a problem for you. The police will look after them, and if they're part of any conspiracy their bosses will find out. They're finding out already. Did you see the faces of them in court? I'd say they got a good hammering already, so there's probably a good chance that there'll be no evidence against you from them.'

When I started to ask something he said, 'Hold on. We have to look at the worst, and the worst is that they'll all go into the witness box and testify that you did it. That's what we have to watch. If it comes to that. If they find a body. Big ifs.'

He went on. 'Then there's the two sisters. Nearly loony, I'd say. Wouldn't be able to give strong evidence, even to save their own skins. Although witnesses like that are often the most damning. Still, we should be all right there, I could put a fair amount of pressure on them in the witness box; I knew their father. Now that leaves the O'Mara woman, Willie Rank and Henry Mac and Scarry and yourself, is that nine?' He counted on his fingers, puffing through his nose and moustache.

'How much do you know about the O'Mara woman? How long have you known her?'

I told him all the details, the meeting on the road, the meal at Henry's, the bath, the drinking, the sharing a bed with her that night, then her coming to see me, her bruises.

'We could ask for her to be medically examined,' he said. I also told him about her terror.

He said, 'And you're sure you never met her before? She's very well-known about these parts. And her own parts too.' He laughed at his joke. I said I had never met her before.

'Did you do the bold thing? I have to ask. In case they put it to you in the witness box.'

'No. Nothing. I didn't. 'Twasn't for want of the invitation from her. But I didn't. I never did with anybody.'

'Well, regrettably, Mr Newman, medical science hasn't yet found a way of proving a man's virginity. If it had, well, a lot of façades would collapse, wouldn't they? But you see the problem – who will believe that you were in the same bed with her and didn't?'

'I know.'

'How and ever, I reckon I can have a go at her in the witness box, I'd say she's a bit hysterical. Now that leaves us with two right geniuses. Rank. And McCracken. Did you know either of them before?'

'No.'

'So you're an unknown quantity to them?'

'Well, I don't know. Henry Mac seemed to know a lot about me.'

'He's a fright in that direction. He makes it his business to know about everyone. He's a bloody spy, that fellow, always getting information – and using it. He'd have made it his business ever since to find out all he could about you. He's the one that worries me. He's very plausible. He'd be a great witness, and his accent would make a jury think he was a nob. He's a problem. And as for Rank – I think I'll do a bit of detective work. He needs discrediting.'

I told him about Rosaleen's remark that 'Rank was in some deal or other that the Postman knew about.'

'I bet he is. He's in everything, all of it dirty.' He

finished taking notes.

'Well, Mr Newman, I can tell you that whatever you think yourself, apart from not reporting the accident to the police, and that's what it was when you left the scene according to yourself, an accident – apart from that failure to report an accident – mind you, so far it's only me that thinks it – you haven't put a foot wrong in terms of the legal aspects. Their ploy is going to be to give the impression that if any foul play is done you were at the root of it. Now they'll do that in the hope of transferring all the suspicion and blame on to you – one culprit suits everybody far more than nine, easier to hang one than nine, d'you follow me? But none of this might happen at all, because, don't you see, the police have a problem. First of all there's a conflict of evidence, your word against eight of them. And most of all there's no body, so there might be no inquest. There's going to be one devil of a job making a murder stick if there's no body. And if there's any kind of efficient hush-up, they'll conveniently ignore your statement – oh, they'll test it first, in every direction, by accusing you, or by accepting what you say, but there's a right conundrum on the loose here. And another thing – there's an awful row blowing up over the way those two policemen appeared in court, all bruised and beaten up. They were given the works by a senior officer, a notorious hard man who was called in from Headquarters by the local Superintendent. Known as "the Bull". A brute. A thoroughgoing, vicious brute.'

I shivered and asked him, 'What will I do?'

'You're to do nothing. Just remember everything. Have you a copy of your statement? Well, learn it off by heart; that is your story and if you stick to it the truth will come out. Of course, there's another thing. If there's no body, and if there's a conflict of evidence in the statements, and if they can't prove anything, no blood-stains or fingerprints on you, for instance, or on any of the others, then the whole thing might go up in smoke.'

I said, 'Isn't that naïve?'

'Ah dear Christ, will you look at who's talking about naïve?'

He left, and, though he was the first ray of hope I had seen, I felt depressed. Could the truth be powerful enough?

We went back to court a week later. In the meantime Mr Hennessy had come to see me and said, 'Things are looking up. The way I said. They're having a hell of a job making anything stick. Without the body, like I said. Has anyone come to see you?'

'No. Nobody. Just the warders, and the prison gover-nor came to see if I was all right. Oh, and the detective who arrested me. He asked me again if I had anything more to add. I said I hadn't.'

'He's not supposed to do that. Have you seen any of the others?'

I said, 'No, we seem to be kept apart.'

'I thought that. Divide and conquer.'

In court he made a great plea for bail on my behalf, and argued that I should be freed without having to put a penny down. The other lawyers all argued for bail; quite a heated session. The judge refused bail for everyone, but told the prosecution that he would only grant a remand in custody for another two weeks, in the absence of more detailed evidence from the police or the expectation of it.

We had a meeting afterwards, Hennessy and I – he

asked for it – and we were given a private room in the back of the courthouse. His moustache was covered in brown snuff stains and he was swearing again. He told me that he had a number of important things to tell me, the most important of which was that it was notable that no evidence of any kind had been taken so far, other than my statement – which to his astonishment had not been introduced into the court proceedings. He also said it definitely looked as if the others might be going to combine and throw the blame on me, and that they had all told the police that I was the culprit, that 'Rank's network', as he called it, was working well. But they had not yet made statements, so they might be gambling upon the conflict of evidence. 'And Rank's friends in high places in the Government are creating a stink, saying their man could never be involved in anything like that, don't we know his seed, breed and generation and aren't they all decent people. You know the sort of stuff.'

He then said the noise I heard was the crowds out in the streets asking for the release of Rank and the others, all shouting that the police had no right to hold on to people without evidence, they should drop the charges. He said it was a most peculiar case altogether, that on the one hand the people were distressed at the disappearance of the Postman, while on the other they were ready to riot in order to have the arrested people released.

'Typical ambivalence,' he said, and he launched into a rant – about the country, Kennedy, patriotism, politics, the Presidential Election, the referendum on proportional representation, the heatwave, the farmers. 'The only good thing to say is that this case is getting political and you might get out on the back of that.'

105

'Oh, I don't want that,' I said.

'You'd prefer a length of hemp, I suppose, a rope? Is that it? Don't be an ape,' he said and launched into another tirade, this time about there being 'more than one kind of hypocrisy'.

When he calmed a little and returned to the facts of the matter, he said he thought the police were now getting desperate to find the body, that without a body they were in a pickle, that they were under pressure from HQ, the Government was asking questions and that they were in a right fix because on the one hand all the other suspects were blaming me, and on the other hand my story was the one the local police seemed themselves inclined to believe.

'So realistically, in law itself, I may be in a – relatively safe position?'

'Well, there's nothing happening and no news is good news.'

We came back from the court in the usual manner, the others in a police van, while I travelled in a police car: divide and conquer. But something had changed. I was handcuffed, for the first time, and nobody in the car spoke to me. They ignored me. When we got to the prison I had been moved to a different cell, much more isolated. The light bulb had been taken out, and none of my possessions had been transferred.

'What's this about?' I asked. No answer; they slammed the door. All evening, all night, nobody came, no food, no water, nothing. Nobody came to take me to exercise; no contact with the warders, nothing, no food later, no heating came on. These walls were two feet thick. I had no watch, there was no sound. Dead silence. I began to feel as if I did not exist.

The morning came and – if I had been asleep – I woke.

I stood up, stretched, used the bucket in the corner, shook the door a little, shouted, 'What about my breakfast?'

No reply.

I shouted and shouted.

No reply. Not a sound of any kind, not a human voice, not a clatter, not a tick or a tock.

All day this continued. A tiny window ten feet above me, not much bigger than a cigarette packet, gave light. I tried to do exercises, leg stretches, arm swings, things I tried to remember from school. I sang.

Oh my Dark Rosaleen, do not sigh do not weep.

The priests are on the ocean green. They march along the deep.

There's wine from the Royal Pope upon the ocean green
And Spanish ale will give you hope, my Dark Rosaleen.

It came out well, sweet and mellow, better than I could have expected. Then I burst into tears. For the first time. I lay on the pallet, pulled the blanket over my head and cried. Got out of bed, looked in the small thick square mirror, shouted, wept.

Two more days – I think – this lasted, making three days in all. No food, no water, no light, and finally no sleep. My mind swung from one state to another, joy to suicide. I recalled every hurt and every snub of childhood and after. To get rid of the feelings, to bomb the emotions out of me, I took the most frantic exercise, pretending I was not hungry, pretending I was not thirsty, and eventually I pretended to myself that I was asleep.

I dreamed that I stood on the edge of a field with some

people, and that this entire field was covered by a huge gentle golden orb, most of which lay beneath the surface and curved just a little above the ground and glowed from within. It had been covered by a tarpaulin, and where the weather had torn holes in the black canvas the golden light flowed through in patches. One of the women in the small party with me, tall, with curls turned in all round her shoulder-length hair and a small black hat like an advertisement featuring an American secretary, began to walk on this vast gentle golden lighted dome, and even though she wore high heeled shoes they only sank soft and wrinkly into the lovely surface of the orb, they never penetrated or punctured it. A man in the group called out to her not to walk on it, that she would tear it with her heels, and I said reassuringly, 'No, no, that is quite all right. Quite all right. That, you see, is my soul, and it is impervious to spikes or to being trodden upon.' The light from the dome glowed brighter and brighter, then it flashed, then there was a bang, terribly loud, terribly bright. The noise came from my head, and a strong light shone in my eyes A large fist hit the side of my head, like a vicious accident. A hand pulled me up by my hair. 'Get up. Up. Up. Up. Upupup.' Such roaring. I was lifted bodily out of the bed by the hair and flung against the far wall, which I crashed into with force and just managed to stay standing. Not a thing could I see, the light was flashing right into my eyes, blinding, hurting. The figure came towards me again. No dream. The fist hit me again on the left temple and sent me reeling. I fell, flat on the floor, and a boot was placed in the middle of my back, 'This could break your rotten spine, you murdering little pig,' the same voice shouted, and again yelled, 'Up. Up. Up. Upupupupupupupup-upupupupup. UP.' As I stood, the fist hit the back of my head and I was shoved forward, then pushed face-first into the wall. I barely managed to protect myself with my hands in front of me. I was grabbed by the hair again and rushed backwards and tripped by the same huge boot. I lay on the floor, not responding to the cries of 'Up' and the figure came down beside me and said quietly 'You – will – get – up. When the Bull tells you to get up you get up.'

The Bull. Oh, Jesus.

He grabbed my ear, twisted me straight up and I staggered. 'Stand still.' Deafening. Blinding.

A fist crashed against my head, knocked me off balance. 'I said – Stand still!' The huge fist hit me again. The light shone straight in my eyes and was then switched off. The cell was in absolute darkness. I was blind. And total silence. Was he still there? I had my eyes closed. I could hear no breathing other than my own rasping, half-crying breath and muttering. This went on for ages. I stood, somewhere in the cell – I had lost my bearings. My trousers began to grow cold: I had wet them. Without warning another blow landed on the side of my head and I reeled. The light came on again and the huge hand grabbed my hair from behind and turned me and said, 'Run. Run.' I was run across the cell, the door slammed open, then out into the corridor and hard up against a wall. A blindfold was squeezed over my eyes, tight. Other hands grabbed me and the voice said, 'Run, Run.' Then I was galloped along the corridor, and if I stopped or tried to stop I was struck. This all happened in silence. When we stopped I was forced to face the wall.

My head was struck again, I shouted and a hand came over my mouth with such force that I felt a tooth loosen. 'Do that again and I'll break your jaw,' said the voice of the Bull. Then I was dragged, half-lifted down another corridor, into night air, bundled into a car which drove off, fast. I half-sat, half-sprawled across the back seat, and beside me sat another figure. From the size it must have been the Bull. 'Now, Mister-Expert-on-Mine-Shafts, we'll test your expertise.'

I said, 'I know nothing about mineshafts.'

'Oh, don't you? What were you doing up at the mineshafts early in the morning a while back?'

'Nothing.'

'Oh, you were there, were you?'

My eyes were hurting under the blindfold. 'Back at the scene of the crime, were you? Little pig.'

I said nothing.

'Answer me, you little pig.' The fist descended again, this time on the back of my head. I said nothing. Silence fell, but for the gear changes, and the drone of the car.

After a long drive the car stopped, the doors opened. I could hear the sea, and the bliss of the sound made me almost forget my hunger and pain and humiliation. A rope was tied around my arms and chest, locking my arms down by my sides, wound about several times, tied under my arms too, around my waist, a complete trussing. Several torches flashed and suddenly I was being dragged up a slope at a run. The Bull was shouting 'Run him, run him,' and on and on they ran, with me half-falling, being kicked, hitting my shins and legs off stones, falling into wet grass on my face. Once they stopped and an argument was conducted in low voices. I thought I heard the words, 'Want him to live, for Jesus's sake.' Then we set off again, this time at a trot.

We stopped. For several minutes. They moved away. The ground was very cold. They came back; I heard their feet swishing in the wet grass.

I was lifted bodily off my feet, straight up in the air like a perpendicular column. Then the air grew chiller and I felt myself held over the edge of something, a precipice. 'The blindfold, take off the blindfold,' said the Bull. The blindfold was taken off, the torches shone all around me, and I could begin to see that I lay on the edge of a hole rimmed with brick. The edge of a mineshaft.

A boot pushed my shoulder and I fell into the hole, then was brought up with a jerk as the rope bit into my shoulders. Much shouting from the top. I dangled for a moment, banging off the sides, was dropped again at great speed, then brought up again with a jerk. The Bull shouted, 'Is he down there? Is that where you threw him? Would you like to join him?' Again they dropped me at speed. I kept my eyes shut, tried to close my mind. Then I hit water, and screamed, took in water with the scream, gurgled.

At last they began to haul me up. The gulp of air made me cough. Again and again, face, knees, shoulders, head banged out of control against the brick sides of the damp shaft.

Down three more shafts they did this, the Bull and the two or three others – whom I never saw either – running me across the ground roped, and then lowering me in jerks up and down. Sometimes I hit water, sometimes not. The Bull shouted all the time. 'Where is he? Where is he? Can you smell him? How would you like to rot with him?'

At one point, my mind, my consciousness obviously began to go, and they hauled me back up and lay me on the ground. Then, when I seemed to be recovering, the Bull again pushed me and I fell down the shaft, down, down, down this brick tube so far this time and so fast that I thought this was the end – until the rope brought me up short again. This time I still wore the blindfold which, oddly, made it worse. The next thing I remember was the seat of the car, the door open, my legs sticking out, someone undoing my ropes.

For a moment I thought I was rescued, as a soothing voice said, 'Is that better?'

I said, 'Yes', and then another blow landed on my head from the other side. The Bull caught my hair and said very slowly, very deliberately, 'Where is he? Where is the body?'

I said, 'Buried,' and passed out again.

I woke in the open air. No blindfold, no ropes, standing up, in a grey light, nobody ahead of me. I could move. I could move my arms. Had they let me go? I turned to look behind me and a fist hit my shoulder, 'No looking – straight ahead.' We stood in a village graveyard, a church over there, several old leaning headstones covered with moss, just enough early light to see.

'Walk,' said the Bull. I walked, straight ahead.

'Is this the place? Is this where he's buried?'

'I don't know. I don't know.'

'We'll find out.'

We stopped by a recent grave.

'No flowers,' said the Bull. 'No wreaths – but you didn't give him any, did you? Is this his grave?'

'I don't know.' I was crying like a small boy.

'We'll find out.'

A shovel was put in my hand. 'Dig.' Then another car drew up, and other men appeared, among them the two policemen, Bill and Kit, who came into Connon's that night, who had been arrested, were also in court, so bruised and cowed. They had shovels too.

I began to dig first, peeling back the clods and stacking them in some sort of system.

'He's done this before,' said the Bull.

The three shovels moved the earth quickly and soon struck something. I cleared the earth away from it. The shiny wood had begun to rot.

'Open it.'

'No.'

'Open – the – coffin.' He kicked me.

I placed the edge of the shovel's blade under the lid of the coffin and lifted it. It came away easily, breaking as it did. The burial had been recent. The person had been buried in clothes, not a shroud. To my relief, if I could call it that, it wasn't the Postman, but a woman – judging from the hair an elderly woman. The flesh had begun to rot on her face; in the light of the torch I could see some movement on the bridge of her nose, ooze on her cheekbones, the clothing still in good condition, the crucifix of the rosary held at the breast, green and white decomposition on the clasped fingers.

'Not him,' said the Bull. 'Give her a kiss anyway.' He shoved me with his boot into the grave. I managed not to fall the full way but as I started to clamber out he said, 'I said – give her a kiss.'

One of the other men said, 'Ah, Jesus, sir.'

The Bull said, 'Shut up.' And to me, 'Give her a kiss, or do I have to force you?' I started screaming and continued to scramble out. He grabbed my hair and forced me down, down, down, pressing my crouching back with his boot until I fell face down upon the decomposing corpse, my face connecting with the hair and the jaw. Another hand hauled me up.

The Bull had not yet finished. We dug another recent, unmarked grave in that cemetery. This time the body was more decayed, almost skeletal, the clothes falling away. Again a woman, her mouth grinning. This time the body was drier, dust only, the odour not so bad. This time we did not fill in the grave.

Into the car again. Across country fast as the morning brightened. Same procedure. This time he asked me to shake hands with the corpse, and though his men argued against him they did so too late to prevent my automatic, terrified response. Her clammy hand more or less came off in mine. Then the smell became unbearable, rotting flesh, decomposed toes, slime on my hand.

I half woke up in the car. At the prison gate I was handed over to a warder and taken to a different cell, my old one. The warder helped me to undress, called another, and a doctor appeared. Commotion began. Some time later, perhaps a day, perhaps two days, I don't know how long, the prison governor came into the infirmary. Stood at the end of my bed. 'Is there anything you want?'

I said, 'No, thank you.'

He said, 'Your solicitor, surely?'

'Not yet.'

'Some fruit?'

Hennessy arrived. He said, 'I came two days ago, but they wouldn't let me see you. They said you had a collapse. Jesus, look at you. What happened?'

I told him. He made notes. When I came to the part about the graves he looked incredulous. I said, 'It's easy to check. I think it was Kilross graveyard, one of them, anyway.'

He said, 'Sure, easy to check. Not that I'm doubting you. But we can use this. This is mighty stuff. We have them now. This is national, this is. I think you're home and dry, now. This makes it really political and the wrong way round for them.'

'Even though I never saw them?'

'Even though you never saw them. Look, there's warders' evidence, and there's governor's evidence, that you were out of here, and there's the doctor's evidence who examined you. They won't go against all that. They'll have to issue details of the Bull's movements and duties if we ask them. And what about the two policemen? Sure they're in a mess too.'

'They'll cover up some way.'

'They won't. They can't. Not now.'

He came back the following day. He said, 'There's a new scandal in the papers – grave-robbers.' And he laughed out loud. 'You were right, Kilross was one of the graveyards you visited.' Then he said, 'I think we'll have a deal.'

I said, 'No deal.'

'What?'

'No. The truth of this must come out.'

'Oh yes, oh yes,' he soothed me. 'But we have to get you out of jail first.'

'And how are you going to do that?'

'Well, you're back in court next week. They've put out a story about you having had a nervous collapse, the judge gave extra time. The police'll be falling over themselves to see me right. We'll be pressing for a complete acquittal. The police are our only opposition, and they're not going to oppose. In fact they're saying you won't even need to be in court. Do they want you telling your story in the witness box? No siree.'

'Is that the wisest course?'

In fact, it took four more weeks. I was ready to go to court long before that, but they wanted all the bandages off, all the worst bruises, the obvious ones, face and head and hands, healed. And Hennessy couldn't hurry it up. The police delayed and delayed, told the judge it was likely they might not bring charges but they just wanted a little more time and because they said they were unlikely to bring charges, the judge went along with them. Obviously some very tricky stuff had gone on.

We drove to Craven Court for the last time, the others in a van, me in a police car, though this time I sat alone in the back. And I never appeared in court. The police offered no evidence. Hennessy reported back to me that the two policemen were missing, as was Rosaleen. They were represented. The judge discharged everybody.

The Agent came down the stairs from the Public Gallery, and Mr Hennessy.

'We'll slip out a side door and get away from that crowd and from the others. We can go over to the bank and have a cup of tea.' Outside, believe it or not, Rank was making a speech. From behind the curtains of the

Agent's house, I watched. They actually lifted Rank, shoulder-high, to the The Enterprise where Affectionate Pat waited at the door, beaming, his bald head shining.

Epilogue

I love September. There's an old wives' tale that says you most enjoy the season you were born in. The sun has well and truly lodged in the west, no red sky tonight, cold tomorrow. I got out of the car a few moments ago, just to stretch my legs, walk up and down a little. I feel older, ages older. Some brave soul tried a swim on the strand half an hour ago; the cold got to him – just as well, before the tides and rip-currents did. How high is this cliff? Through the green water below I can see the flat rocks of the sea-shelf beneath. The tides here run wild and hard, would whip a body down to the Azores in no time.

Head Office said take a long holiday; I said I want to be around for a bit, unfinished business. Hennessy told the Agent in that case it might be as well if I 'hid' somewhere. I have been staying several miles away, down the coast, in a bungalow owned by the Agent's wife's sister. I have it to myself. I figure that since 'they' might not expect me to stay in the area, nobody – as Hennessy said – would look for me down there. I may soon be back at work; the bank has considered my case, the bank doctor even took a look at me. I've been walking a lot, out far by the waves' edge. And writing this record of events – for whom? Who knows?

Mr Hennessy tried to talk me out of what I said I wanted to do.

'You can't go the whole hog. Leave it lie.'

'Why can't I bring a private prosecution?'

'Oh, you can. But you shouldn't. Tricky. And dangerous. You saw what you're up against. Don't.'

'I am determined to.'

He said, 'If you do somebody will get hanged.'

'But will it be me?'

'Probably not. But you know full well you're running up against some very powerful people. Anyway, why do you want to do it?'

I said, 'I was brought up to believe that this country could be a good place to live in. I was brought up to think that now that we had our own Government and independence, people would behave. These people are covering up the death of a man. Not murder maybe, I am prepared to accept that Rank didn't mean to kill him, that the fall was what did the damage – if he was dead at all when they buried him. But covering up to save their own skins is not the spirit we deserve for gaining our independence.'

He lowered an enormous mouthful of the whiskey he had brought and he tore into me. We were sitting on the verandah.

'Listen. When are you going to come into the real world? You're a prig, that's what you are. And do you know what a prig is? A prig is a pain in the arse, that's what a prig is. You should grow up. This nonsense you have about this country. What makes you think that just because a few gunmen became heroes and shot up a few convoys of lorries and eventually forced out a regime who were sick of being here in the first place – what makes you think those fellas wouldn't become as venal as hyenas? This country isn't about heroics, this is about

119

graft. The Risen People are no better nor no worse than anyone else in the world, as crooked as a ram's horn, and trying to turn a buck or two. Jesus Christ, man, cop on to yourself. Your Dark Rosaleen that you sing about, she isn't a mystic wronged woman, she's a whore they all ride the arse off of now, that's who she is.'

He coughed. 'Let me tell you something. This country is at a junction the likes of which it never saw before. I grant you there was a kind of an innocence that you picked up, a kind of euphoria after the Revolution and Independence and the Civil War and the Treaty and all that shebang. And I grant you that it was right to a certain degree to think of – what was it? "the laughter of comely maidens", wasn't that it? But that's all over, boy. The comely maidens are wearing face-powder and slacks now. This is nineteen-fifty-nine, not nineteen-twenty-two. Fair enough. You learned it in school. And right that you should. But if you think that what you're going to see is some kind of rustic Utopia you're on a loser. I'm telling you – the only way you'll get anywhere is by looking at the reality, and the reality is that these people would rather set up a conspiracy of silence to save their own skins than come clean about something that might have been no more than an unfortunate accident. That's not patriotism. That's shit – that's what that is. But 'tis natural – the way shit is natural.'

'But,' I said, 'this is corruption.'

'Sure it's corruption. But sit tight, boy, if you want to see corruption. Have you heard the news from the States? Kennedy is definitely going for the Presidency. Now if he gets in – 'tis then you'll see corruption. The minute Kennedy gets into the White House they'll find another reason to hide their graft under some new kind of myth, because they'll drag in every patriotic and sentimental shibboleth they can get their hands on, and the one sure thing you can know in this country is the minute you hear somebody speaking of our great traditions and our sad emigrations and our fight for freedom, there, my man, you have corruption. This place is only beginning.'

I said, 'We were taught in school that the men who fought in the Revolution were –'

'Oh, don't talk about the men who fought in the Revolution. That went down the Swanee a long time ago. Forget that for a bunch of hey-jumbo. Look at the crowd you're saying you'll take on here. Look at Rank. He's ripping this country off the whole time, on the grounds that his father was shot in the Revolution. Yeeh-hah, that genius would steal the milk out of your tea and come back for the sugar.'

'But that's no reason for not taking them on.'

'Maybe not. But there's a more practical reason for not taking them on.'

'What's that?'

'A billhook in your scrotum, that's what. So grow up, Mr Newman. Anyway it's not all bad. Look at the Election. They threw out the PR thing even though they re-elected the Chief.'

'Did you see the thing in the paper – he sent a message of "deepest filial devotion" to the Pope,' I said.

'And why wouldn't he? Sure he wasn't doing anything else at the time.'

He poured another drink as I said, 'I don't know. I still feel I should take them on. Someone should. Someone should shout stop.'

'Oh, I agree with you. And that's why, God help me, I'll help you. But I'm hoping you won't.'

'But if I don't – who will?'

'I take your point. But the tide is against you.'

'How do you mean?'

'Look. Add it up. There's this country, just showing a bit of prosperity, people are begining to own cars, a bit of land, a bit of education. There's enough now going round for people to see it and want it – or for them that have it to want more. Now there's still an idealism, the kind you're talking about. Only – and this is the point – only it's been turned commercial. The Risen People want to rise further. They want to rise to the fur coat and the big car. Great. Who doesn't? Who can blame them? And when they see Kennedy, a child of their own, there you go. Up she flew and the cock flattened her, as my father used to say. They'll all think they can do it. But there's a thing in there that's the most dangerous of all. There's a sick weakness. Rank has it. And here's what it is. Along with the greed, there's that old foolish pride, that thing you call patriotism. The Dark Rosaleen merchants who tell you in the pub late at night or after Mass on a Sunday morning, "The country is still unfree". You can hear them singing it. And it won't be long until there'll be a new bunch of cowboys with their guns banging away along the Border. They were at it three years ago, in 'fifty-six, weren't they? And already they have ballads out of it. Well, the greedy ones, the ones you're trying to fight – they'll create the climate to let the gunmen in. Give it ten years, by which time we'll have a national underbelly as soft and flabby as an old sow, the tits dry from everyone sucking at them. Then the boys with the new ideals will be in – concealed or disguised as only Christ knows what, or riding on the backs of some well-meaning bunch of agitators or liberals or whatever. They'll be at it hammer and tongs, and there won't be anyone down here with enough gumption to stop them because their own old nonsense, that same, sickly, sentimental republicanism, will mesmerise us. Only this time it will be lethal.'

He sat back, getting drunk. 'Just you watch out. You'll see. This cover-up, Larry Dwyer's, is only one. By the way there's another, an almost identical case – another postman too, dead, over the west, in Ballinlow – and they can't find him either. No witnesses there either. I wonder why it's always postmen? Ah, yes, once Kennedy hits this country, that's the furrow opened. Now – why don't you give up?'

'I can't. Or at least I don't think I can.'

'Well,' he said, 'I'll start the work, so, but people will find out soon.'

Awful coincidence. The bungalow next door – only two on this stretch of beach – is owned, it transpires, by the Teacher's married sister. Of course, different name, nobody twigged, an untidy, scrappy bungalow in need of care, another holiday house like this one, but not as well-tended.

Three evenings ago our jaws dropped mutually as we came out on to the identical front verandahs overlooking the ocean, the Teacher and I, and saw each other. Last night he knocked at my door, Eugene Scarry.

I didn't let him come in.

'I have a message for you. Henry and Willie Rank want to meet you. They want to meet you to discuss things.'

'Nothing to discuss,' I said.

'You should,' he said. 'You should. I'll bring them here tomorrow night.'

'Do not.' He was gone.

They came, at dusk. Trust Henry to pick the most impressive time. At first I did not answer the door, then Henry called through the letterbox, 'Mr Newman, we mean no harm. We know you're there, we saw your car outside.'

I opened the door a little.

'How many of you?'

'Only the two. The Senator and myself. Eugene didn't want to come.'

Rank, running a hand over the wavy hair-oil, said he was sorry about 'the misunderstanding' over the billhook.

'Misunderstanding,' I shouted. 'He nearly cut my balls off.'

'Yes, yes,' said Henry. 'Everybody got much too excited in this altogether, much too excited. We all panicked.'

'That's a laugh, Henry, you panicking.' I wasn't afraid of him any more.

'What is it you want?' I asked.

'We want your silence,' said Henry.

'No.'

'We'll buy it.'

'No.'

124

'Why not?'

'Too much at stake.'

'Such as?'

'Such as – the truth. A widow. Two children. A principle.'

'The widow is well looked after,' said Rank. 'And the children.'

'I'll bet.'

'As for the principle,' said Henry, 'can't you find other principles you can exercise just as enjoyably?'

'Think about it,' said Rank.

'We can take care of you,' said Henry – an ambiguous remark that made me shiver.

'And take your time,' Henry continued. 'Take twenty-four, take forty-eight hours.' He seemed ageless in this drab room.

Rank stood up, pulled at his white raincoat so that it stretched tight around him and began to leave. 'I'll wait for you outside, Henry.'

Henry turned to me and said, 'Rosaleen said to say good-bye to you.'

'Why? Where's she going?'

'She's gone away for a while. Meet us the evening after tomorrow, Saturday, around this time. It'll be all right, I assure you. You have my word.'

'Where? Here?'

Putty in this man's hands after all, despite my brief bravado.

'No. Make it easier for you to talk. Neutral ground. And somewhere we won't be seen. Do you know the Old Point?'

'Can I bring somebody with me?'

125

'No. Why compromise yourself?'

Which is how I come to be here, sitting back into the car now, looking at the sea. In the distance I can hear the noise of the carnival, the funfair, that comes scruffy and freshly painted to these small towns every summer. One of the sideshows contains a booth with a crane; if your coin is successful you can manipulate the crane so it will pick up something, some cheap treat, and drop it through a hole, down a chute, into your waiting hand. I have never won a thing from it. The lights have just come on in the funfair, I hear tin music on the wind.

Here they come. In the mirror I see a car driving up behind me, Henry. Driven by Led. Driven by Led. The man who killed his own little child with his own terrible hands. They stop fifty yards away. I look back, I start the engine. In doing so I see too late the other car which comes from the front, three men in it, Rank and his two men. It parks broadside across the road. Rank gets out and I see in the dusk his thin white raincoat flapping like a phantom. I shall sit tight for a moment or two, and think.

The priests are on the ocean green. They march along the deep.